For eight years now *Per*
to be the world's top-s
Originally published in
series has now appeared
the States.
Over five hundred *Perry*
Continent and *Perry Rho*
annually. The first *Perry*
Space', has now also been released in Europe.
The series has sold over *140 million* copies in Europe alone.

Also available in the *Perry Rhodan* series

ENTERPRISE STARDUST

THE RADIANT DOME

INVASION FROM SPACE

Kurt Mahr & W. W. Shols

Perry Rhodan 3

Galactic Alarm

Futura Publications Limited
An Orbit Book

An Orbit Book

First published in Great Britain in 1974
by Futura Publications Limited

The series was created by Walter Ernsting and Karl-Herbert Scheer, and translated and edited by Wendayne Ackerman.

ISBN 0 8600 7804 3
Printed in Great Britain by
Hazell Watson & Viney Ltd
Aylesbury, Bucks

Futura Publications Limited
49 Poland Street,
London W1A 2LG

GALACTIC ALARM

CHAPTER ONE

"You won't be able to understand that! You will be unable to comprehend any of the impulses. Your brain will become utterly confused, and you—"

Thora stopped short without completing her sentence. The words would not come as fast as her frantic mind demanded.

How simple it is to see through her game, thought Perry Rhodan. *It is not my brain she is worried about. Her real concern is to convince me that I am not yet sufficiently developed to grasp her secrets.*

"What difference does it make to you?" he countered. "What would you lose in me? And the sight of Rhodan as a babbling idiot should give you a lot of satisfaction. Or am I mistaken?"

She was aware that he was trying to throw her on the wrong track, and it particularly annoyed her that he seemed to succeed so easily.

"That isn't the point at all," she replied tersely. "The psychotapes can be played only a certain number of times, and we must be careful not to exhaust them unnecessarily—especially in this case, where failure is so clearly indicated."

Rhodan extended his right hand in a pleading manner. "But you do me wrong, Thora," he said. "Haven't we managed so far to understand everything that's been presented to us?"

Thora snapped her fingers with disdain. "Whatever you have learned before is nothing compared with what you will be faced with now!"

Rhodan turned around to look at Khrest, whose face bore the usual serious expression. One had to know him well to recognize from the way the skin on his forehead was moving how much Khrest was actually enjoying this.

I would gladly exchange 1,000 fictitious programs for a single situation like this, thought Khrest. *Lord of all the universes! The most intelligent of all Arkonide women and a demigod of the human species . . . and behaving like little children!*

But in reality there were quite serious things at stake here. After some initial resistance, Thora had no longer objected when the two members of the "underdeveloped human race" received instruction, via the hypnoschooling method, in some of the achievements of the superior Arkonide sciences. But now she offered strong resistance to their demand to open up the last secrets of the aliens' treasury of highest knowledge. She deeply distrusted Rhodan's argument that this would increase his efficiency.

Khrest supported Rhodan in his plea. He explained to Thora that the Arkonides' last hope lay in the inherent energy of the underdeveloped human race and the assistance they were giving to the two survivors of the Arkonide space expedition. This help could be increased many times if Rhodan and his friend were given the necessary scientific information.

In the end Khrest had to make use of the authority he had over Thora in his capacity as a member of the ruling Arkonide dynasty, before he could break her violent resistance to Rhodan's request.

Rhodan had been affected by Thora's obstinacy more than he cared to admit even to himself. He expressed his gratitude to both aliens at the conclusion of the discussion.

"Thanks for your confidence in my friend Bell and myself. It won't be wasted on us," he told Khrest. Turning to Thora he added, "As time goes on you will come to believe that I harbor no thoughts that would be detrimental to you or that would hurt your pride."

Rhodan felt he needed to add this last remark for Thora's benefit, although he was well aware that Thora was none too receptive to such declarations of good faith. Not yet at least.

"Go to hell!" exclaimed Reginald Bell with deep conviction.

At the same time he tried to hide the fear he had felt when Tako Kakuta suddenly materialized out of the void close to him.

Tako was all smiles. His round, boyish face glowed with pleasure.

"Why to hell?" he asked in his high voice. "I deserve a better fate. I am bringing you good news."

"Good news?" echoed Bell. "Where on Earth would it come from?"

"From Tai-tiang," smiled Tako. "He has finally understood that he can't do any harm to the Third Power, even with his pioneer divisions. His troops are withdrawing."

This was exactly what Bell had expected would happen after Tai-tiang's unsuccessful attempt to penetrate the Third Power's domain. Tai had dug an underground tunnel to avoid the protecting energy dome around Rhodan's base. As soon as he reached a position immediately underneath the center of the base, he intended to place a hydrogen bomb there and detonate it, blowing up the Third Power's command center with all its crew. But before Tai-tiang's forces could even bring the bomb inside the underground shaft, Rhodan had sealed off the tunnel with the help of powerful Arkonide instruments. Thus, Tai-tiang's plans of destruction had been foiled.

But still Bell found it reassuring to hear Tako's report of Tai-tiang's withdrawal. "Thanks, Tako," he sighed softly with relief.

"So long, sir," said Tako, and disappeared.

Bell kept staring at the spot where Tako had stood just a moment before. In the past few months he had come to believe that anything amazing and shocking was to be expected only from the Arkonides. Therefore, it would take quite a while for him to get used to the idea that Tako Kakuta was not an alien Arkonide but a member of the human race, even though, being a teleporter, Tako could suddenly appear out of thin air next to him and vanish just as swiftly as he had come.

Reginald Bell was thinking about the extraordinary gift of teleportation, which seemed altogether unbelievable to him despite Tako's daily demonstrations. To Bell it seemed on the same order of incredibility as a horse being capable of human speech. A slight hum interrupted Bell's thoughts, and he glanced over to the wall, where the soft glow of a telecom screen lit up the cool twilight of his room.

Rhodan's face became visible on the screen. "I would like to discuss something with you, Reg," said Rhodan. "Are you busy now?"

"I have always time for you, my friend! Where? In your cabin?"

"Yes. Khrest is here with me."

Bell nodded briefly and left the room. Behind him the video screen grew dark. As soon as Bell entered his friend's cabin, Rhodan declared, "We plan to leave Earth for a few days."

Bell listened attentively as Khrest continued the explanations. "We must leave Earth in order to be totally undisturbed when we administer the rest of the hypnotraining to you two. But besides guaranteeing absolute quiet for you, this trip serves still another purpose."

The Arkonide scientist's eyes seemed to light up with a faint degree of excitement as he continued, "We assume that our spaceship on the moon was not completely destroyed. I can't believe that terrestrial rockets could be that powerful. I am confident that we will manage to rescue a number of important items, if we take enough time out for such a mission with this trip."

They decided to start their trip within the next forty-eight hours. In the meantime a feverish activity ensued, making the corridors of the vessel resound with the hurried steps of the crew, especially Rhodan and Bell.

The Arkonide auxiliary vessel that had brought Thora down to Earth from the moon on her initial rescue mission was well supplied with a group of robots whose special function was to repair anything that was out of order. But in Rhodan's eyes their inactivity between repair jobs seemed a waste of their usefulness. Any second the robots spent in the storerooms was a luxury that Rhodan felt they could ill afford. Therefore, he suggested to Khrest that they work out a programmed activity schedule for the robots.

"How soon will you be able to finish such a program?" inquired Rhodan.

"In ten minutes."

"Ten minutes!" Rhodan could not conceal his admiration.

Khrest confirmed his words with a brief nod and turned to his desk. As Rhodan left the room he quickly noted the time.

Lost in thought as he hurried down the hallway, he failed to notice that someone was approaching from the opposite direction. As he impetuously made a sudden turn around the corner he collided head on with Thora.

"Oh, I'm so sorry!" he said with an embarrassed smile.

She seemed to be in a good mood. She looked at him with mild irony. "If you grow still more energetic, maybe someday you will be able to look around corners and see what's coming."

"And if you could someday walk with your nose not quite so high in the air, you might be considered an attractive female!" he replied.

Thora bit her lip and left him abruptly, soon disappearing behind another bend in the corridor. With a sigh Rhodan continued on his way.

Soon Rhodan rejoined Tako Kakuta, who had been waiting for him. Rhodan handed him a sheaf of papers on which he had made some notes.

"Will you look through these, please, Tako? Later we can discuss them together."

"Yes, sir."

Tako began to read the papers at once, while Perry remained a little longer before returning to Khrest's workroom.

"You are just in time," the Arkonide scientist greeted him. "I have just finished."

Together they left and took an elevator down to the storeroom where the robots had their quarters.

"I have worked out a program for each of them," said Khrest, not without pride. "You will be amazed to see what the machines will have accomplished by the time we return from our trip."

In the storeroom there were about twenty robots with different functions. The Arkonides had not permitted themselves the luxury of constructing them in their own likeness. These were no toys to them, after all; these were machines with work to do. So most of the robots looked like machines mounted on Caterpillar tracks. Rhodan noticed that they also possessed claws that enabled them to lift themselves up and over obstacles that could not be overcome by the tracks alone.

The schedule Khrest had worked out for each of the machines was on a paper thin strip of plastic. "These strips contain all necessary impulses," declared Khrest.

Then he began to feed the programs into the robot machines by inserting the plastic strip into a slot at a different place on each of the twenty robots. Khrest waited until the machine began to hum, which was the signal that it was now ready to work, as it devoured the plastic strip.

"After such a long period of inactivity," explained Khrest, "it will take a few seconds for the activation to take effect."

A few seconds seemed to Rhodan a ridiculously short span of time, considering the feverish activity the robots displayed within a few moments.

Humming like bees, they began to leave their places and move about, carefully avoiding any collisions with each other. Then they all marched toward the elevator in which Khrest and Rhodan had arrived just a little while earlier. Rhodan burst out laughing after the last machine had left the storeroom on its way in the elevator.

"I'll be twonked!" he groaned. "I'd never have believed such a thing possible!"

"You will be really amazed to see what these robots are capable of," answered Khrest. "They are true robots. Up to a certain degree they can think and act and make decisions on their own. I can't imagine what would have become of our Arkonide civilization without them.

The robots did not leave the ship immediately. First they collected all the items they had been instructed by their programmed schedule to take along with them to the outside.

When Rhodan had first made plans to effect the task he had set himself, he had been obsessed with the idea that no time must be wasted. Rhodan saw a chance that was worthwhile taking if he could procure from terrestrial industry the various parts needed to construct a faster than light spaceship with an unlimited radius of action. All that was necessary was to place the parts in exactly detailed order. Their assembly would have to take place inside the protective energy bell. In view of the political situation of the great powers, as well as the character of mankind in general, it would have been an irresponsible risk to permit the factories of the world's population to proceed with the construction of the spaceship itself.

Rhodan knew that the space inside the energy dome was sufficiently large to complete the assembly of the starship. But he had never assumed that it could be accomplished within an area of less than thirty square miles.

He watched with enthusiasm the nonstop activity and purposeful behavior with which the robots went about their task. After they had unloaded everything they would need from the space sphere, they stacked all items neatly at a distant spot and set out to level the ground.

There was no doubt in Rhodan's mind that they would have completed a greater part of the necessary work by the time he, Bell and Khrest returned from their trip to the moon.

Tako had finished reading the notes Rhodan had left him. When Rhodan returned to Tako's cabin, the Japanese was sitting thoughtfully in his chair.

"Did you understand everything?" Rhodan asked.

"Yes, sir. It won't be easy."

Rhodan pulled up a chair and sat down beside Tako. "Listen, Tako," he began urgently, "we are up against a serious and difficult job. If we want to retain the two Arkonides as our allies, we are forced to build a ship for them that has the action radius they need. Unless we can bring them back to their own home planet and then have them return here with us, we shall be very, very old men before we accomplish anything the world can respect. We need Khrest's help, and to get his fullest assistance we must have the right spaceship."

"Yes, sir. I do understand," said Tako.

"They will always be after you," continued Rhodan. "The secret services of the different countries will pursue you, and you will constantly have to be on the alert. You will find many people who want to do business with us because of the money, and they will be ready to supply us with anything we need. But there will be also those who will make fabulous offers to you and then inform the police as soon as you turn your back. Never rely on your special talent alone. It will take about five to six days for the secret service to find out that you are a teleporter. From then on they will shoot first and then ask questions. They will lay traps for you and then try to finish you off."

Rhodan bent his head closer to the intently listening Japanese as he concluded, "We will supply you with an Arkonide protective suit. That should be of great help to you. But you will carry the final responsibility for your own safety."

Tako nodded resolutely. "Yes, sir. I understand."

"It will be up to you where you want to start with your job. Perhaps you might do best to approach private industry. I will give you a list of all the things we need before you leave. Khrest says that such a spaceship must have a diameter of at least 1,000 feet. There will be many people who will think you crazy to order scaffolding for a 1,000 foot high plastic structure, or fusion generators with a capacity of 100 million megawatts. In addition you must be careful not to place too many orders for certain parts with one firm; otherwise, they might guess what they are intended for.

"You must not have any illusions—this is the most taxing task that anyone has ever asked you to carry out. You have until we are ready to start on our trip to prepare yourself for it."

Rhodan got up. Tako rose and bowed low. Rhodan smiled and cordially slapped his back.

"Lots of luck, Tako. A great deal depends on your success."

Rhodan was busy making a list of the things that Tako was supposed to get for them. There were many items, and Tako would have to find them within a short time.

Of course, man's industry would not be able to supply the faster than light drive. Khrest hoped to find the necessary components inside the remains of the destroyed vessel on the moon. The rest of the parts they required to construct the spaceship would have to be acquired separately and then assembled here inside the base of the Third Power.

Rhodan was seized by a feeling of utmost excitement when he pondered what would happen within the next seventy hours. He would learn the secrets of the faster than light drive!

He was startled out of his thoughts by the sudden arrival of Bell, who raced into Rhodan's cabin without even knocking. Bell was upset, and he was out of breath, as if he had been running at top speed to get here.

"Klein has sent the signal!" he said quickly. "We must send Tako to him."

"Klein?"

"I think we should hurry up. Klein won't care to crawl too long out there in the hot desert sand under the eyes of Tai-tiang," urged Bell.

Rhodan flipped the switch for the telecom. Tako's smiling face appeared on the video screen.

"Reg will explain to you what we want, Tako."

Bell took over. "Klein has given the arranged signal. OPQ on the 6.3 megahertz band. He is waiting for you at the previously arranged rendezvous. Please hurry!"

"Yes, sir," Tako said quickly. He did not even bother to switch off his telecom, and Rhodan and Bell saw how he vanished from the spot where he had just been standing.

Lieutenant Klein was a triple agent. First, he was an agent for the International Intelligence Agency—this was his profession. Second, he was an agent for peace and international understanding—this was his inner personal conviction. And third, he was an agent of the Third Power, whose ally on the outside he had become. Klein, together with his colleagues Kosnow the Russian and Li the Chinese, had joined Tai-tiang's troops in their withdrawal after their unsuccessful attempt on Rhodan's base. But now Klein had risked leaving the safety of the military camp and was advancing again close to the wall of the energy screen around the Third Power's base. He must have a very valid reason for it.

Klein had prearranged several codes for his meetings with Rhodan's people. Each code designated a specific rendezvous spot, and "OPQ" on the 6.3 megahertz band meant a small hill about three and a half miles southwest of the southern shore of the Goshun salt lake.

Hardly fifteen minutes had passed before Tako rematerialized. Rhodan and Bell had been staring at their intercom screen to observe Tako's reappearance in his room. But instead he chose to appear right in Rhodan's cabin.

Bell turned around, startled by Tako's unexpected coming.

Tako paid no attention to him but addressed Rhodan in an unusually excited manner. "Bad news, sir. Peking has ordered all branches of the nationalized industrial enterprises to inform their secret service at once about any of our agents. Moscow has given the same instructions to their manufacturers. And inside the NATO countries severe penalties have been announced threatening any industrial concern entering into dealings with us."

Rhodan seemed to be staring at something in the air.

"Some sly fox must have found out about our plans," Tako said.

Rhodan advanced two steps, then turned suddenly on his heel and looked straight at the Japanese. "Tako! Nothing will be changed as far as your job is concerned. I am afraid, though, that you will have to proceed even more cautiously."

CHAPTER TWO

The craft started to the moon according to plan. The robots had been busy for two days; slowly their mapped out work began to take shape.

Enough field generators had been left behind in the Gobi Desert base to maintain the energy dome while the ship was away. Still, the moon flight vessel had taken along several of the instruments needed to foil the plans of the Third Power's military adversaries, who had started to prepare strategic maneuvers against them as soon as they learned that the Arkonide vessel had set out on its lunar trip.

There was no work to be done during the flight. The automatic guidance system of the ship functioned according to the instructions preset by Khrest.

When they were about 300 miles from Earth, the ship's radar system showed the first approaching enemy rocket. A few seconds later the rocket became visible as a flitting metallic arrow on the videoscreen of the direct optical observation instrument. Rhodan felt fear surge through him and could hardly catch his breath for some moments as he became aware of the ball of fire released by the exploding rocket. Only after realizing that their own ship had not been affected by the holocaust could he relax again. The Arkonide space sphere sped away from Earth with increasing velocity.

Rhodan turned around. Bell, who had been standing behind him, looked at his former commander with a sheepish smile. "That's something like Christmas or being promoted suddenly," he said with a still uncertain voice that could hardly conceal the fright he had experienced a moment ago.

Khrest merely smiled in his enigmatic but friendly way. Thora did not react at all. She simply stared as before at the video screen.

Another series of rocket attacks followed, at an altitude between 500 and 2,000 miles above Earth. The protective energy screen around the Arkonide craft warded off fifteen enemy rockets altogether, and the ship's crew did not notice even the slightest jolt.

Then the bombardment ceased.

The ship went into orbit around Earth at a distance of 8,000 miles above the planet's surface.

"Now we can start with the hypnotraining," said Khrest. "You saw with your own eyes that the rockets cannot harm us at all. Even if they should resume their bombardment, it would not disturb you during your schooling."

Rhodan gave his consent to begin the hypnotraining. As soon as the overwhelming fear of a direct rocket hit had abated, he was seized once again with excitement, anxious to find out the last secrets of Arkonide scientific knowledge.

The procedure was the same they had experienced already several times previously. Rhodan and Bell lay on a comfortable couch while they were connected to the information transmitters.

"It will take about three hours," explained Khrest. "This time we are dealing with extremely difficult material—difficult even for me."

He checked all connections again and asked, "Ready?"

"Ready!" replied Rhodan and Bell simultaneously.

Rhodan lost consciousness while he was wondering why Thora had not come to watch. Never would he be able to describe what he felt during the hypnotraining session. All he could remember later was a swarm of disconnected bits of information that made no sense. He no longer had any bodily sensations. All that was taking place now seemed to occur exclusively in his brain. But without the posthypnotic influence that would eventually render this schooling process effective, he could not have made any use of the various isolated items of newfound knowledge that he could still recall.

He knew that his brain would be given a period of adjustment after the conclusion of the hypnoschooling. His mind needed the rest to recuperate from the superhuman strain. He remembered that after every previous training session he had awakened refreshed and feeling wonderfully alert.

When he regained consciousness with a splitting headache this time, he realized at once that something unforeseen must have interfered with the schooling process.

Khrest was standing at Rhodan's cot gazing at him with an expression full of helplessness and uncertainty.

Rhodan was fully alert in an instant. "What's happened?" he asked the Arkonide scientist abruptly.

Rhodan could hear the moaning of his friend Bell lying next to him, but he paid no attention to it. Bell would need the usual few moments to regain full awareness.

Khrest jerked convulsively. "Are you feeling . . . ?"

"Yes, I am feeling splendid! What's the matter?"

Rhodan felt anything but splendid. His headache was unbearable.

"Thora . . ." stammered Khrest. "She has . . ."

Rhodan remembered that he had feared something of the

kind. Thora had too quickly consented to their plan to conclude the last stages of their hypnotraining. He should have realized sooner that she had something up her sleeve.

He rose and tore away the leads connecting him with the transmitter. Khrest recoiled as if in terror. Rhodan was amazed at the scientist's reaction. Why should Khrest be suddenly afraid of him? He wondered.

"Where is Thora?" snapped Rhodan.

"In the command center," replied Khrest meekly.

Rhodan no longer paid any attention to Khrest. The last thing he heard as he stormed out of the room was Bell's gruff voice, saying, "Go ahead, chief! I'll follow right away."

Rhodan hurried along the corridor that led to the center of the ship. He pulled his small Grinnell gun out of his belt. He regretted for a moment that he was not carrying one of the Arkonide weapons in addition to his usual protection. The small caliber bullets would hardly make a dent in the locked Arkonide door leading into the command center, where Thora was hiding.

She had locked the door indeed, as he had suspected. She was not going to run any risks with these two Earthlings, whose uncanny urge for activity, measured by Arkonide standards, had frightened her repeatedly.

Rhodan activated the audio communication system inside the cabin. No answer! He followed by hammering with his bare fists against the door. There was still no sign of life from the inside. He walked back a few steps to the nearest telecom outlet. He pushed the command center button and waited impatiently until the video screen lit up.

Thora had been waiting for his call. Her face filled the screen. Rhodan was startled to see such fierce hatred in her eyes. Never had he encountered such violent and raw hate in the eyes of any being.

"What is going on? What do you want?" she inquired calmly.

Rhodan knew that it would be useless to shout at her. The method of communication that seemed to work best with her was a display of superiority on his part. He could disarm her if he made her understand that he considered her no match for him.

"What kind of nonsense have you been up to this time?" he asked her with a quiet grin.

She appeared to have steeled herself against this kind of approach. He could perceive nothing of the narrowing of her eyes that usually indicated how much she was hurt by his sarcasm.

She addressed him in her own Arkonide language, to make him understand how much she considered this her very own affair, of no concern to this poor, backward human being. "I am sick and tired of being chased about, you monkeys. That's all."

Before Rhodan had time to reply, he heard his friend Bell approaching from a bend around the corridor. He gave him a sign with his right hand, which was outside the viewing field for Thora, asking him to stay in the background so that Thora would not see him. Bell understood and obeyed.

"Tell me," Rhodan said, resuming his conversation with Thora, "what plan have you hatched up to get rid of us?"

For the first time he could detect some signs of worry in her. "I will land on Earth," she answered, "and take matters into my own hands."

"What matters? Do you really believe for a moment that you can go out and purchase your new spaceship anywhere on Earth, ready made?"

"No, not at all," she replied haughtily. "I will force these humans to build one for me."

"Force them?" laughed Rhodan. "How?"

Thora had stepped back from her video screen so that Rhodan could now look beyond her. Suddenly he knew how he could deter her from her crazy plan.

"You know just as well as I that this ship has enough weapons on board to deal effectively with more than ten of your type of planet."

In the meantime Rhodan had begun a feverish activity that could not be observed by Thora. He had stepped closer to his telecom set, all the while giving signs with his right hand for Bell. He pointed to the floor of the hallway, where it joined the opposite wall.

"I will land inside the energy dome in the desert base on Earth," continued Thora in the meantime, "and make the terrestrial governments understand what I want from them."

Rhodan nodded, and at the same time he continued the hand signals to his friend Bell. His index finger still kept pointing at the same spot as before, while his thumb pointed toward the video screen of the telecom set. Rhodan could not tell whether Bell had grasped what he was trying to tell him.

"I make no secret of my intention to make a heap of ashes out of your planet, if my demands are not obeyed."

"That method guarantees, no doubt, your safe return home to Arkon?" mocked Rhodan. Now his right hand had changed the signal. His thumb pointed upward while his index finger imitated the movement of pulling a gun trigger.

Rhodan broke out in a cold sweat. "Why won't you reason out this problem calmly?" he said, trying not to show his inner tension. "You want to destroy mankind if they won't fulfill your demands. What will that leave you with? What will you do for the rest of your life? Live out your days in a miserable existence on Mars or Venus? Is that the kind of future you want for yourself and Khrest?"

Thora motioned impatiently, as if to shrug off his warning. "You know that mankind won't let it get to the point where they face extinction. I will make it entirely clear to them what they can expect if they don't comply with my wishes. They can't hope for mercy from me."

Rhodan felt hatred surge up in him as he heard these words. "The nations of the world will simply laugh at your requests," he countered ironically. He paused for a moment, full of silent triumph, as he heard Bell creep away quietly behind him. "They will laugh at you, then dig themselves into deep safety shelters, and you still won't know what to do to get help after you have destroyed their world with its industrial potential."

Thora seemed to grow taller as she snorted contemptuously, "Mankind will do nothing of the kind! No one will agree to his own destruction if he can possibly avoid it."

Rhodan was leaning against the wall in a relaxed manner in order to show her that he was willing to have a lengthy discussion with her about this problem. "Well, that is exactly where you have the wrong picture about the human race. Don't build up your hopes too high. Those few cowards among us humans who would rather give in to you than risk their lives would not be of much help to you anyhow."

He still wanted to tell her more, but this very instant he noticed some movement beside her on the video screen. Close to the spot where Thora was standing was an opening of the fresh air duct about the size of a man's head. The air duct was a five foot wide shaft that led vertically throughout the ship, distributing fresh air into every room.

From this opening Rhodan now saw the barrel of a gun emerging, held in a big fist.

"Okay, chief!" said Bell, so loudly that Rhodan could hear him over the intercom. "Turn around, young lady, and raise your hands!"

But Thora could not comply with his command. The first instant she heard Bell's voice she had started to turn around in his direction. But before she completed her turn she was overcome by fright and fainted. She fell to the ground with outstretched arms.

"Great!" bellowed Bell from the air duct opening. "That's exactly the way I wanted it. Now, shoot out the door lock before she comes to again!"

"I'll get something for this from Khrest!" shouted Rhodan, and started down the corridor, calling Khrest's name. Out of breath, he reached the information room, where barely fifteen minutes earlier he and Bell had been lying under the influence of the hypno transmitter.

Khrest was already at the door.

"Let me have one of your weapons," panted Rhodan. "One that can shoot out the lock of the command center door. Thora locked herself in. She has fainted. If we don't hurry she will wake up and everything will have been in vain!"

Khrest spun around and disappeared down the hall. Half a minute later he was back. He was breathing with great effort as he handed Rhodan a heavy needle ray gun. "Here, take this," he urged, "but be careful with it!"

Rhodan raced back down the corridor, all the while getting the weapon ready to shoot. He stopped fifteen feet from the door of the command center and directed the needle thin, invisible energy ray through the visor onto the electronic door lock.

The plastic metal of the door began to hiss, form bubbles and melt. A hole appeared in the heavy door, and as soon as it was sufficiently large Rhodan stopped shooting.

The door no longer offered any resistance as he pushed it open. Rhodan could hear Bell breathing a sigh of relief from the direction of the opening in the air duct. "Thank heavens! I couldn't have shot her."

Rhodan lifted the still unconscious Thora off the ground and placed her gently on one of the couches that lined one side of the wall. He activated the telecom and called Khrest.

"Come here, please. I want you to be present when she regains consciousness."

But the first to appear in the command center was Bell. He had not even stopped long enough to wipe the sweat off his brow. A wide grin spread over his broad face as he stepped through the demolished door.

"You don't know how proud I am that I could figure out your hand signals."

"You are just plain smart," Rhodan complimented him jokingly, putting on a serious air, as if he really meant it.

Khrest arrived just then. "How did you manage that?" he asked, shaking his head in amazement.

Rhodan chuckled. "We discovered the air shaft just in time. Reg took the elevator down to the air conditioning plant and crawled up the shaft. When Thora saw him threatening her with his gun from the opening in the wall she fainted."

Khrest sat down carefully at the edge of the couch on which Thora was resti_g. "I can well imagine that," he said thoughtfully. "I almost died myself when I saw you get up off the hypno couch a little while ago."

"Why should you feel that way?" asked Rhodan.

Khrest waited a few moments before he said, "Way back at the beginning of our hypnotraining technique, when we built the first instruments but lacked the necessary experience to operate them, there occurred several regrettable incidents when the training session had to be interrupted for some reason or other. In every case the person undergoing hypnoschooling lost his mind. We found a simple explanation for this. During the training process the brain is in a condition of extraordinary activation. Unless given the opportunity to return slowly to its state of normal functioning, it becomes short circuited. The result then is a kind of insanity that even our best psychiatrists have been unable to cure."

Khrest paused for a moment and looked first at Rhodan and then at Bell. "Do you realize what I mean by that? Since the first days of hypnotraining there has been no greater crime in Arkon and all worlds that are subject to the Arkonide code of law than interrupting such a training session."

Khrest motioned with his head to the still unconscious Thora. "When you were connected to the transmitter, Thora felt absolutely safe from any interference on your part with what she planned to do. She knew that I would not dare wake you before the end of your schooling period. Those three hours would have been enough for her to return to Earth with the craft and to make all necessary preparations so that you would no longer have posed a threat to her."

He fell silent for a few seconds.

"But you awakened us in spite of that!" interjected Rhodan in a grave voice.

Khrest silently nodded in affirmation, while looking down at the deck. "I assure you that this was not an easy decision to make. But I had to make a choice. Unless I aroused you from your state of unconsciousness, Thora would have landed on Earth and ruined all our efforts. There is no doubt that she would have brought about the destruction of Earth as well as that of this space sphere."

Khrest glanced up again and smiled. "The rest was easy. We were facing death in any case, so why not seize the only chance that presented itself? I was hoping all the while that your human brains would react differently from our own, that they might withstand the shock of having the hypnotraining session interrupted."

Suddenly Khrest's face was all smiles. "And though I was hoping against all odds, my fondest wish came true. Mankind—"

Suddenly he was rudely interrupted. Something began to move behind his back on the couch, and with a voice still feeble, Thora exclaimed furiously, "You are a miserable traitor, Khrest!"

Rhodan jumped up, and Bell leaped across to the foot of the cot. But Khrest remained seated. A sad smile came over his face as he answered quietly, "No, my daughter, I am not a traitor. Someday you will see the light. But I am afraid it will take a long time yet with you."

Thora, exhausted, closed her eyes.

Rhodan gazed at her intently, and when she opened her eyes again she seemed to falter under his severe expression.

"Listen to me!" he said harshly. "We are all fed up with your nonsense, your stubbornness and your disgusting arrogance. Now we shall make sure that you will never again cross our plans before you have learned to use your rational mind."

He seemed to pierce her with his eyes as he went on sternly, "You need not be afraid of us—we won't harm you. But you can rest assured that from now on I take command of this vessel. Any further attempts on your part to try to carry out your foolish notions will be regarded as mutiny."

Thora had nothing to say. Her face remained rigid, and nothing revealed what was going on behind her forehead.

Rhodan made clear to her that she was free to move about, but he gave strict orders to Bell to watch her carefully, as long as he could do so.

Their primary concern was to complete their interrupted hypnoschooling as quickly as possible. Rhodan regretted that they had not taken either Dr. Manoli or the Australian Dr. Haggard along on this trip. They could have kept watch so that nothing could happen to them while they were lying helplessly under the transmitter.

As things stood now, all he could do was to give the needle ray gun back to Khrest and urge him to use the weapon if Thora should make another attempt.

Then Rhodan stretched out again on the transmitter cot and waited patiently until Khrest connected him up once more to the apparatus.

As soon as Khrest had strapped him in, it was Bell's turn. The usual question followed: "Ready?"

And the usual answer was given: "Ready."

And again they were overcome without any transition by the deep unconsciousness of the hypnotraining. It was as if somebody with one well aimed movement had covered up all the universe with a dark, heavy blanket.

CHAPTER THREE

While Tako Kakuta got himself an entirely new wardrobe in one of Pittsburgh's big department stores, his mind was preoccupied with thoughts of the increasingly difficult problem of procuring sufficient financing for the enterprises of the Third Power. Ever since the Arkonide cruiser had been destroyed on the moon, they had sorely felt the lack of enough suitable objects for bartering with Earth's industrial concerns. Their supply had become so scarce that they now had to save just a few items for the most important business transactions.

Tako had managed to reach Pittsburgh without difficulties. Rhodan gave him a free hand in selecting the best spot for carrying out his mission, and Pittsburgh, with its huge industrial concentration, had seemed a good starting point.

Tako was fully aware that he was in a more advantageous position than any other member of the Third Power who happened to be outside the base in the Gobi—nobody knew who he was. No one had the faintest idea that he was working for Rhodan. Tako intended to use this advantage as long as possible. But he would have to drop his convenient anonymity the moment the negotiations started.

As he left the department store Tako glanced with pleasure at his reflection in the store window—young executive type, dressed conservatively in a gray flannel suit. But now the real task must begin. He went to the next taxi stand and directed the driver to take him to a ferroplastic production enterprise that seemed right for his plans.

Ferroplastics, Limited, was part of the big Du Pont concern.

Tako knew how to impress the young lady receptionist. He was ushered in to one of the office managers, who assured him that he would get him an interview right away with one of the directors of the firm.

Tako made it very clear to the young man: "Don't forget to mention that I intend to place a big order!"

He had given a false name, for which he had been supplied with the necessary identification. But he did not indicate where he came from or who his bosses were. Let them believe for the time being that he was an emissary of the Asiatic Federation. It was well-known that the Asiatic Federation was far behind in the field of metal plastics.

Tako waited awhile, stitting near the receptionist's desk in the spacious entrance hall. He seemed absorbed in one of the many magazines that had been placed there for visitors. But his glance was fixed just above the rim of the paper he held in front of his face. This way he could study leisurely what was going on around him. A constant stream of activity filled the huge hall, but there was nothing to cause him any alarm.

Twenty minutes later the young man who had promised to get him to see one of the big bosses reappeared. He grinned. "Mister Lafitte will see you right away. Follow me, please!"

Mister Lafitte's office was on the top floor of the gigantic building. Tako enjoyed the wide view over the city as he was led along a hallway. The young man took him as far as Mr. Lafitte's door, which he held open for Tako.

Mr. Lafitte rose behind his desk as Tako entered and motioned to the young man to leave them alone.

"Have a seat, please!" He motioned toward a chair by his desk.

Tako sank down in the comfortable cushions and politely refused a cigarette that Lafitte offered him from a gold cigarette case. Slowly and casually Tako looked around the luxuriously furnished room. Lafitte grew restless, but that did not seem to bother Tako.

Finally the Japanese glanced up at Lafitte and asked, "Where can we talk business?"

Lafitte seemed nonplussed. "What do you mean? Here, of course! This is my conference room. This is where all my business discussions take place."

Tako just smiled politely. "My mission is of such a difficult and delicate nature that I cannot take the slightest risk whatsoever. I hope you see what I mean. Just look at this pretty vase here. Doesn't it make a marvelous hiding place for an electronic listening device? I fully appreciate your precautionary measures. But therefore, you should understand mine as well."

Lafitte's face ran the gamut from initial uneasy surprise to sudden anger and finally a cunning grin. "Apparently, dear sir," he remarked a bit too smoothly, "your bosses have sent me one of their brighter agents."

He got up from behind his desk, walked around next to Tako's chair and added, "I am willing to carry on negotiations at any place that will suit you. What do you have in mind?"

"Let's meet in my hotel," suggested Tako. "I'll ask them to reserve a conference room for us."

Lafitte pointed to the phone on his desk. Tako placed a call to his hotel and ordered one of their smaller private meeting rooms.

While they were descending in the elevator, Tako closely observed all of Lafitte's moves. There was no indication that he gave a secret order to anyone to follow them. And yet Tako could not help feeling that Lafitte had something up his sleeve that Tako had not foreseen.

The taxi ride to the hotel was uneventful. Tako looked through the rear window several times but could not see anyone following them. If there was a tail, he must be exceedingly skillful. That was one possibility that could not be excluded, thought Tako.

Their conference room was ready. Tako gave orders not to disturb them during their negotiations. They sat down at a small table, and Tako proceeded at once to place Lafitte under the influence of his small hypno set, while he dictated his order.

". . . the wall of a sphere, with a diameter of exactly

1,000 feet, thickness of the wall two and a half feet. Made of ferroplastic A-10 with wolfram additives. To be delivered in easily transportable sections. You will receive further instructions as to the method of delivery.

"Our payment will consist of a so-called degravitator. This apparatus can nullify gravity and counteract any gravitational pull up to ten G's. This valuable instrument will pay more than adequately for the ferroplastics you will supply us.

"It is of utmost importance to observe the exact date of delivery. Either we will be in receipt of the order within four weeks or we will be forced to cancel the order. There will be no written contract. We have full confidence in each other."

Tako stood up. Lafitte stared at him with blank, dim eyes, typical for people under hypnotic influence.

"If it should ever cross your mind that I am an agent of the Third Power," Tako concluded, "you will forget this at once! I am an emissary of the Asiatic Federation, which is quite backward in the field of ferroplastics, as is generally known. The ferroplastic sphere will serve as a housing for a nuclear reactor that is under construction. That is all, Mr. Lafitte. I hope that everything will proceed smoothly and that our order will be filled to our satisfaction. Here are the exact details for delivery."

With this Tako handed Lafitte several typewritten pages that he had painfully composed the previous day on one of the rental typewriters supplied by the hotel.

Tako switched off the hypno set and observed how Lafitte's face gradually regained its normally alert expression.

Lafitte rose from his chair and said with obvious pleasure, "I am glad that we reached this agreement so quickly. I'll propose this matter to our board of directors immediately. I do not foresee any difficulties. After all, we will be more than amply paid for this order."

Tako opened the door of the conference room. The corridor outside was deserted. Bright sunlight entered through a wide window and was mirrored in the highly polished floor.

"Don't forget to inform me at once what decision your board of directors makes. My people are most interested in a speedy delivery. Otherwise, I will be forced to place our order elsewhere."

Lafitte waved his hand and laughed. "Don't you worry! Everything will be in order. You will hear from us by tonight."

Tako accompanied Mr. Lafitte to the elevator. As soon as he descended, Tako rushed to the front window leading to the street and observed Lafitte leaving the hotel, calling a taxi and driving off without once looking back.

Tako waited at the window. One minute later an inconspicuous looking car that had been parked across the street drove off and followed the taxi.

Lost in thought, Tako returned to his room. The gray car that he just had seen was no real proof that anyone had followed Lafitte or shadowed Tako . . . but one could never be absolutely sure.

Back at his room, Tako phoned Ferroplastics, Limited. A pleasant voice answered his call.

"This is Mr. Yakamura calling," said Tako. "I had the honor of discussing a big order with your Mr. Lafitte just a few minutes ago. Mr. Lafitte indicated that he would meet at once with his board of directors. It is quite likely that I will have to get in touch with him shortly in order to supply some further data. Will I be able to reach him directly through you? Will the meeting take place in your building?"

"You can talk to him at a moment's notice," replied the switchboard operator. "I'll connect you directly with the conference room a few doors down the hall from me."

"Thank you so much," said Tako. "You have been most helpful."

Then Tako proceeded to take off his new suit and put on the Arkonide transport outfit that Rhodan had given him to take along on this mission. He hid a gun in his belt, as well as the hypno rod.

The doorman at the hotel entrance viewed Tako's unconventional outfit with obvious displeasure; but Tako was sure that he must be used to all kinds of outlandish costumes worn by exotic guests from primitive countries.

Once again Tako hailed a taxi and asked to be taken to the Ferroplastics, Limited, plant. En route he reexamined his plan for any weak spot. Everything seemed so incredibly simple that Tako began to have doubts about the primitive structure of his own ideas. But he calmed his apprehensions when he recalled the most unusual means at his disposal, which would justify the apparent crudeness of his strategy.

At about the same time, M. V. R. Lafitte was storming through the visitors' waiting room at Ferroplastics, Limited. He had managed to summon the members of the board of directors, and he was confident of obtaining their consent within an hour.

As he passed by the switchboard, Miss Defoe called out to him.

"What do you want?" he asked impatiently. "I'm in a big rush."

"Mr. Yakamura has called. He wanted to know if he could get in touch with the board of directors' meeting through this switchboard."

"Mr. Yakamura?" Lafitte replied with a frown. "What did he want?"

"He just wanted to make sure he could reach you, in case he had to give you any further information regarding the deal while your special meeting was in session."

Lafitte nodded briefly. "That will be fine. Just connect him with the meeting room, if he should . . . Well, what's going on here?"

A tall young man had entered the hall and stopped next to Lafitte, looking rather worried. "I followed your car, as we had arranged. Is everything in order?"

"Yes, Morgan. Everything is in order."

Morgan hesitated. He half-turned to leave but still remained. "Sir, are you really sure that everything is okay?"

Lafitte's fist pounded the switchboard operator's desk in exasperation. "Get off my back! I'm absolutely sure that everything is fine!"

Morgan seemed unconvinced. He just murmured, "Well, if you think so!"

Then Morgan left the visitors' hall and went out to the big stairway leading up to the building entrance, where he had parked his car temporarily. Slowly he drove his car to a shady place in the company's big parking lot. Then he returned quickly to Miss Defoe's desk. Lafitte had left.

"What is this all about, Morgan?" asked Miss Defoe. "What are you afraid of?"

Morgan pulled a chair up to the switchboard and sat next to the operator. He shrugged. "I am not quite sure myself. They seem to have concluded some enormous business deal. Lafitte moved heaven and Earth to get all his board of directors together for a meeting right away."

"I don't know why that should bother you so much."

"Have you ever witnessed the way Lafitte goes about making business deals?"

"No, of course not."

"The bigger the deal the longer he needs to make up his mind. Lafitte has never negotiated for less than five hours. This interview lasted that many minutes before they came to an agreement. Well, maybe it took a quarter of an hour, to be exact. And now he has called this urgent directors' meeting. This means this deal is so enormous that he cannot decide for himself. But to conclude negotiations within fifteen minutes . . . ! That's what bothers me. It just doesn't seem right."

Miss Defoe grimaced. "I wouldn't lose any sleep over it."

But Morgan insisted, "Just let me listen in if this Japanese fellow should call, will you?"

"Oh no, I will do nothing of the kind." Miss Defoe was most indignant at Morgan's request. "I never permit anyone to overhear any conversation."

Yet Morgan won out. He persisted until she reluctantly agreed to his demand.

The two continued with some small talk until the heavy door to the foyer was opened. The noise made Morgan turn around and look at the door. The wide, heavy panel swung outward, then inward, and bounced to and fro until it came to its original position of rest again. Morgan wiped his eyes, as if trying to erase this unbelievable picture; but the picture did not change. There was the usual hustle and bustle in the busy foyer, but nobody could be seen near the door.

Miss Defoe noticed his uneasiness. "Now what's the matter?"

"The door opened by itself, but nobody came in!"

The phone rang. Miss Defoe answered. Then she turned her attention back to Morgan. "You are ready for your vacation, Morgan. You're beginning to see ghosts in broad daylight."

But in this moment something strange occurred. An office boy was crossing the hall, carrying a pile of papers. Suddenly he stopped, as if he had collided with an invisible obstacle. He dropped the papers and threw his arms up in alarm, screaming.

Morgan rushed over to his side. "What's going on?"

The boy's face was distorted with fear. He was trembling, and his words came slowly. "I . . . he . . . there was somebody . . . something . . . and I bumped into it! Just here, right on this spot."

Morgan stepped over to the spot the boy had pointed to. "Nonsense!" he snorted. "There is nothing here!"

The boy shook his head, still frightened.

"Well, so what was it?" asked Morgan.

"I really can't say for sure what it was. It could have been a man; but he did not wear a regular suit. It felt hard to the touch."

Morgan scratched his head. "Didn't you see anything?"

"No! That's just it!"

"Well, just forget it." Morgan bent down and helped the boy pick up the scattered papers. "Just forget the whole thing. I wouldn't mention it to anyone. They'll only think you are seeing things that aren't there."

"Thank you, sir," muttered the boy, and continued on his way.

Morgan went back to Miss Defoe's desk.

"What was wrong with him?" she asked.

"He collided with an invisible man."

Miss Defoe began to laugh hysterically.

"I wonder if he was really imagining things or . . ." Morgan said seriously and with emphasis.

She stared at him incredulously and stopped laughing. "You don't mean to say that . . ."

He did not reply. He cupped his face in his hands and sat there thinking.

A few moments later the door swung open again, but

this time two of the members of the board of directors walked through. They seemed to be in a great hurry.

They passed the switchboard, talking to each other animatedly. Morgan followed them with his eyes. The two men walked over to a double swinging glass door that led to a short, wide hallway from which the conference room could be reached. Morgan saw clearly how both men passed through the glass door. The left wing closed again at once while the right side remained opened for a few seconds. The two men had walked down the corridor a few steps before the right wing swung back again.

There was no doubt in Morgan's mind that some invisible person had followed the two directors through that double glass door. He was just going to alarm the guards. But then he realized that he had no real proof of his suspicions. No one would believe him. They would just laugh at him.

No, if anything could be done, he was the one to do it. It was now up to him alone.

It was plain to see how proud Lafitte was to have entered negotiations for such a fabulous deal. With incredible self-assurance he elaborated to his board of directors about the offer. He did not seem to notice that the faces of his listeners grew longer and angrier by the minute.

Finally Whitmore rose abruptly, sending his chair sliding back halfway to the wall. "In my capacity as the presiding officer of this board of directors, I want to express my deep concern at this strange offer you have presented to us, Mr. Lafitte."

Whitmore's face had turned beet red with anger, and he shouted furiously, "What kind of a joke is this, Mr. Lafitte, to have each of us interrupt whatever we were doing, rush over here and then tell us about this idiotic order somebody wants to place with us! How dare you act so irresponsibly!"

Whitmore seemed near apoplexy; his face took on a bluish tinge. "Stand up, Lafitte! Explain yourself! Otherwise, we will be forced to take measures that would be rather unpleasant for you. You deserve to be taught a lesson that you won't soon forget!"

Whitmore turned around to retrieve his chair and was

just about to sit down again, to listen to Lafitte's explanation, when suddenly something seemed to occur to him.

"Hold your horses, not so fast!" He waved to Lafitte to take his seat again. "What did you say the buyer was offering to pay us for this order?"

"They will give us a so-called degravitator." Lafitte repeated his previous explanation of the conditions of the sale. "An instrument that can nullify gravity up to ten times the gravitational pull of Earth. An ideal means for transporting heavy loads, which can't be matched by anything we have so far at our disposal."

Whitmore seemed pleased with this elucidation. "Well, that sounds quite reasonable, gentlemen." He nodded with obvious satisfaction, looking at his colleagues sitting around the conference table. "If this is what the buyers intend to pay, then these terms seem most acceptable to us. Don't you agree, gentlemen?"

Everyone in the room nodded approvingly. Any memory was wiped clean from their minds that but half a minute ago they had considered Lafitte's suggestions a stupid joke. It did not occur to anyone to inquire who could offer such an instrument, which so far had been dreamed of only in the wildest imaginations of scientific inventors. Suddenly it was sufficient for the board of directors that someone had offered to supply such an apparatus. There was not the slightest doubt in their minds about the absolute sincerity of their customer.

Lafitte read out the terms of delivery, and everyone agreed that they were most reasonable and easy to carry out.

Just as Lafitte had promised, the meeting lasted barely an hour. The offer was accepted, and the necessary instructions for the various department heads were given out at once. The members of the board of directors congratulated each other on having concluded the most advantageous deal in the whole history of Ferroplastics, Limited.

The man who had assisted them in making this momentous decision waited until all the directors had left the conference room. Since he no longer needed to have all the energies of his body at his instant complete disposal—as indeed had been the case when he had started to exert his hypnotic influence on the members of the board—he now preferred not to return the same way he had entered the building. He wanted to avoid causing another unpleasant incident. Therefore, he concentrated his thoughts on a lot near a rather empty street corner in the vicinity of the Ferroplastics building and transplanted himself there with a telejump.

Exactly the way he had visualized it, he landed on a weed covered lot near the Ferroplastics works. No one could have observed his sudden appearance out of nowhere.

Tako walked down the street and waited until an empty taxi came along. A few minutes later the taxi deposited him in front of his hotel. Lost in thought, he walked by the hotel desk without even looking up and got into the elevator that took him up to his floor.

He was very well pleased with the result of his day's work.

The only thing that worried him was that he had been unable to avoid bumping into the office boy since half a second before he had had to step back to avoid someone else. He had not failed to notice that the tall young man who had come to the office boy's assistance had believed more in the boy's account than Tako liked. It looked as if there was now someone who would follow him like a bloodhound; and if he was sufficiently unprejudiced to accept the story of an invisible man with whom the office boy had collided, this person might turn out to become a rather dangerous opponent.

Tako had got a good look at his face and remembered it well. He planned to submit the man to the influence of the hypnorod as soon as he could find the opportunity.

CHAPTER FOUR

Tako opened the door of his hotel room and entered. He had almost reached the table on which he had placed his new suit, when he heard a voice coming from behind him. "Don't get scared, mister. I won't do you any harm."

Tako spun around swiftly, eyes narrowed, and with lightning speed drew his gun, ready to shoot if necessary.

He saw an older man sitting in an armchair near the door. The man had raised his arms when he saw the gun pointed at him. His face had turned deathly pale in fright.

"For heaven's sake," he panted, "put that thing away, please! I am unarmed."

Tako lowered the barrel of his gun. "Who are you? What are you doing in my room?"

"It doesn't matter who I am in this case. I am nothing but a figurehead in this game. I have been sent here to deliver you a message. Call me Webster, if you want to."

Tako examined the old man. He was dressed a trifle too flashy for his age; he did not make a very reliable impression.

"What is the message you have for me?"

"Listen! We know that you want to get various things that will cost you a lot of effort and also might be quite dangerous for you. We offer to act as go-betweens for you and promise to supply you with anything you want to purchase."

Grinning and pleased with himself, the old man leaned back in his chair. "For a price, of course!" he added slyly.

Tako looked at him and pondered. But before he could ask anything, Webster quickly leaned forward in his chair and said hastily, "Before I forget—we are aware that you have a bag of tricks at your disposal. You can probably influence me and force me to tell you all I know. But this won't do you any good. First of all, I don't know the man behind the scenes, the boss. Furthermore, he would interpret your tricks as a kind of vote of no confidence and break off negotiations at once. But if you want to deal fairly with us and pay us well, you will find us to be the most loyal partners you can wish for."

"Who is 'we'?" asked Tako.

Webster shrugged. "Sorry, I really can't tell you, because I don't know myself."

Tako was frowning. He dropped into a chair across from Webster's. "How did you get into my room?" he asked.

"Oh, dear . . ." Webster grinned with obvious amusement

at Tako's naïveté. "There are a thousand ways for an experienced man to get into any room."

"All right, then. I am willing to listen to your proposal. Where do I have to go hear it?"

"This is the address. But wait!" Webster pulled back the slip of paper that Tako was about to take from his hand. "Let me tell you once more—no tricks whatsoever, mister. We will subject you to a thorough examination before we start dealing with you. We are running great risks even offering to have dealings with you. We must minimize that risk as much as possible. Do you get me?"

He held out the address to Tako. "This offer is good for ten days. If you are willing to accept, then call this number and say, 'Holloway will come at 2 P.M.' or '8 A.M.' whichever time will be more convenient for you. Is that clear?"

Tako smiled. "You won't have to wait long for me, Webster."

Webster took his leave. He left behind a rather perplexed Tako. What Webster had referred to as "tricks" were probably the extraordinary feats he could accomplish with the help of the Arkonide suit. But how could anyone have found out about them?

At the same time he was wondering about Webster's personality. There was no doubt that Webster belonged to the lower social classes. The way he dressed and his mannerisms clearly indicated this. But who had sent him, who was behind all this? The kind of answer he'd given when asked how he had entered his room seemed to indicate that he must be a burglar or something of the kind. Could a burglary ring be of any help to Tako in his mission? Did they intend to steal for him all the necessary equipment for a 1,000 foot long spaceship?

This thought was so amusing to Tako that he regained his self-assurance. He had nothing to be afraid of! Nothing as long as he was wearing the Arkonide suit and was capable of teleportation.

Therefore, he did not even bother to change clothes for dinner. Dressed in his Arkonide suit, he went down to the dining room and completely ignored the surprised looks the other guests sent in his direction.

Webster entered a room that contained nothing but a table and two chairs. On the table were a telephone and an intercom set.

Webster carefully closed the door behind him, after he had switched on the light. Then he pushed a button on the intercom. A little lamp lit up, and a droning voice inquired, "What is it?"

"Webster speaking. I think he will come."

"Good. Anything else?"

"No."

"I have something to tell you, Webster."

"Go ahead!"

"Finch has found out some guy who is spying on that Jap. His name is Morgan, and he works for Ferroplastics, Limited. He is one of their house dicks. You will have to help Finch keep an eye on that guy till Yakamura has finished his business with us. We can't afford to have some idiot stick his nose into our affairs. No need to be gentle with him—anything goes!"

"Okay, boss," Webster replied.

"I want something else from you. Connect the intercom with the phone. I want to hear if the Jap should call."

"Will do, boss!"

Webster pushed a button at the base of the telephone.

"Finch has his headquarters in Fratellini's Cafeteria. Hurry up and get there as quick as you can."

"Right away, boss."

"Get going. That's all for today."

Webster switched off the intercom and took a pistol from the table drawer. Then he walked to the door, turned off the light and left the room.

He walked through an office with a row of writing desks and chairs. Everything was covered with a thick layer of dust. A door led to the outside.

The Eastern Transport Co. was a fictitious firm that existed only on a big sign on the office door. Anyone who wished to place an order with the firm would be politely informed that the firm was completely filled up with orders for the next six to eight weeks and could therefore not accept any new orders.

The outside door opened on the thirtieth floor of a modern office building. The hallway was deserted at this hour. Quietly Webster walked to the elevator and took it to the ground floor. He waved a friendly hello to the doorman, hailed a taxi and drove off to Seventh Avenue to Fratellini's Cafeteria. Finch was sitting in a special room that Fratellini reserved for his special customers.

Webster sat down across from Finch.

Finch glared up. "It looks as if the fish has just slipped through the net!" he said slowly.

Jesse Morgan had a great deal to do with the temporary defeat that Finch's people had suffered. Morgan was a Pinkerton trained man who was working for Ferroplastics, Limited. He possessed all the good qualities typical of Pinkerton detectives.

It had not taken him long to find out that he was being shadowed constantly while he was trying to get close to the elusive Mr. Yakamura. He noted that several people took turns following him, and all of them seemed experts at their job.

It was quite an effort to shake these bloodhounds. It took several taxi trips, two movie tickets, a huge milkshake, which he unfortunately did not even have time to taste, and some strenuous muscular effort while racing through some side streets and around corners. But finally he managed to get rid of them.

Still, this cops and robbers chase foiled his original intention to get to Yakamura's hotel room, at least for this evening.

He tried to figure out who these pursuers might be. But since Lafitte had not found it necessary to inform him about the peculiarities of the Japanese, Morgan considered this affair something to satisfy his own private curiosity. If any beneficial results for Ferroplastics, Limited, should ensue, they would be of only secondary interest to him.

Morgan had rather definite ideas concerning the identity of the Japanese. Until a few weeks ago, when a sudden lull occurred, the newspapers had been full of reports about the strange events in the Gobi Desert caused by the people who called themselves the Third Power. Many of these news items had become distorted, exaggerated and altered during their transit from Chinese to American news agencies—so much so that the U.S. papers were full of half truths that even quite unprejudiced readers would shrug off as ridiculous. Morgan, though, was capable of extracting from such reports the facts based on reality. In this particular case, therefore, it seemed highly probable to him that Yakamura was not acting on behalf of the Asiatic Federation, as Lafitte had revealed in some hints, but rather as an agent of this Third Power.

Such an agent, speculated Morgan in his ignorance, would be liable to fall for a cheap trick he had planned.

As soon as he was absolutely sure that he was no longer being followed, he entered a coffee shop, sat down way in the back and ordered a cup of coffee.

After a few minutes he got up and went to the phone booth and closed the door to make sure no one could listen in to what he had to say.

He dialed the number of the Atlantic Hotel, where Yakamura was staying. "This is Robert Donovan calling. I would like to talk to Mr. Yakamura."

"Just a moment, please. I'll connect you with Mr. Yakamura's room."

After a little while a high pitched voice answered the phone. "Hello."

"My name is Donovan," announced Morgan in slow and distinct tones. "I would like to present an offer."

Yakamura seemed to be taken by surprise, to be at a loss for words. But then he inquired, "Who do you presume is interested in your offer?"

"You, Mr. Yakamura, of course! I have many valuable connections, and everything you would have a hard time locating and purchasing, I could get for you in no time!"

"And why would you do such a thing?" came Yakamura's sarcastic reply. "Out of sheer love for your fellow man?"

"No, sir. There is a price for everything."

"So what do you suggest?" asked Yakamura.

"Why not get together and talk things over?"

"Where?"

"You say where," answered Morgan.

After thinking it over for a moment or two, Yakamura

spoke up. "I don't know this place. Let's say we'll meet in a little bar down the street from the Atlantic Hotel, to the left."

"That sounds fine to me. When?"

"One hour from now."

"Very good, Mr. Yakamura."

The Japanese hung up. Morgan could not repress a smile of satisfaction as he left the phone booth.

No one who did not have rather unusal and effective resources at his disposal would have fallen for such an obvious trick. Morgan did not doubt that Yakamura must be sure of an attempt to get him, although he had promised to come. The Japanese must therefore be very sure of himself and his protective means to walk into such a trap.

Morgan paid for his coffee and started to walk over to the little bar for his rendezvous. Although there was still another hour to go, he wanted to arrive there well before the Japanese.

Finch received two bits of news almost simultaneously. The first report worried him; the second pleased him.

"Pete says that the Japanese fellow is leaving his hotel just now," he remarked with obvious annoyance to Webster. Then his face lit up, and he added, "But Vale has found that Ferroplastics dick again. He is sitting in a bar on Washington Boulevard, down the road from the Atlantic Hotel."

Webster gazed at Finch with concentration.

"I think it's about time to teach that fellow a lesson," said Finch. "How about it, Webster?"

Webster rose to his feet. "That's fine with me. Do you have any suggestions?"

Finch scratched the back of his head. "Get him to come out of the bar under some pretext and then drive him out somewhere and beat him up. Tell him that the next time he'll get more than that if he doesn't stop interfering with us. He must keep his nose out of our affairs!"

"Will do, Finch."

Webster left and took a taxi to Washington Boulevard. When he saw one of Finch's people waiting near the curb, he asked the driver to stop. He paid and got out of the taxi.

"Where is he?" he asked Vale.

Vale pointed with his thumb over his shoulder. "In there."

Webster looked down the street. He knew that the Atlantic Hotel was just a couple of blocks down the road. He did not like the idea. It occurred to him that the Ferroplastics detective might have an appointment with the Japanese right here in this little bar.

Webster's fears were suddenly confirmed when he saw the Japanese coming out of the hotel and leisurely walking down the boulevard. He kept stopping in front of store windows to look at the displays. This gave Webster a chance for some quick action.

Where is your car?" he asked Vale.

Vale motioned to an old Ford parked in front of the entrance to the bar.

"Try to detain the Japanese, if he should get here too soon!" snapped Webster, and then ran into the bar.

He knew what Morgan looked like and recognized him at once. Without hurry he walked over to his table, trying to figure out some excuse that would arouse the lease suspicion in Morgan.

Morgan glanced up at Webster. "What do you want?"

"Mr. Yakamura would like to talk to you."

Morgan seemed surprised. "Why, of course. Isn't he coming here?"

The same instant Morgan felt like a fool; he could have bitten off his tongue. How could he be sure that this man had really been sent by Yakamura?

Webster felt relieved at hearing this information and seized the opportunity that had been so thoughtlessly presented to him. "No, he can't come here, unfortunately. But he would like you to meet him at his hotel."

Morgan did not reply. He just stared at Webster, who grew impatient.

"Mr. Yakamura seemed to be in a great hurry when he sent me over here to ask you to come to his hotel. He has to leave Pittsburgh by tonight, sooner than he thought."

"Oh, that's it." Morgan seemed to accept this explanation. He motioned to the waitress and paid his bill. Webster walked out with him.

"My car is parked right here in front. It will be quicker this way."

"No, thank you," Morgan declined cautiously. "I'd rather walk over to the Atlantic, it's so close."

But in the meantime Webster managed to pin him against Vale's car at the curb. Unnoticed by the passersby, Webster had pulled his gun and pushed it against Morgan's ribs.

"Do as I tell you!" he ordered. With a fast glance he noticed that Vale had accosted Yakamura and was busy talking to him.

"Open the car door and get in!" ordered Webster.

Morgan obeyed. He had no choice with the cold steel of Webster's gun barrel punctuating his words.

Webster sat down next to Morgan. Vale was still busy with the Japanese. Webster ground his teeth impatiently. Vale was doing too good a job delaying Yakamura. Webster rolled down the window and whistled to Vale. Vale tried to leave, but with a stubbornness that exasperated Webster, the Japanese stayed glued to Vale. Cold sweat covered Webster's forehead.

Finally Webster heard Vale's words. "Have fun, sir. I'm sorry, but I absolutely have to leave now."

Vale ran over to the driver's side of the car. But Yakamura, who could not be deterred by such brusk leavetaking, approached the car from the curb and peered in. He had discovered Morgan before Vale managed to start the engine. As the motor started, Webster snapped, "Get going!"

But before Vale had a chance to obey this command, Yakamura said in a strangely compelling voice through the half-opened window, "Hold it! I want to come along with you!"

Webster hesitated, unsure of himself.

"You can be reached at AN 2-3551, if I am not mistaken," continued the Japanese.

Webster nodded impulsively.

"Then you'd better take me along. I would not like anything to happen to this young man here. I can make sure of his loyalty in a much more effective way!"

"Okay. Get in, sir!"

Yakamura opened the front door and sat down next to Vale.

"Where did you want to go to?" the Japanese asked Webster.

"Just the nearest way out of town."

"That suits me fine," remarked Yakamura agreeably. "Go ahead!"

Vale drove off. Soon he reached the freeway that led to the outskirts of the city. Soon after that Vale left the freeway and drove onto a sparsely traveled side road leading into some fields. About a mile from the freeway he stopped the car.

"Not yet," ordered Yakamura. "Drive on a bit farther."

Vale looked at the Japanese and then at Webster. Webster just shrugged helplessly.

Vale started the car again and drove for another two miles.

"Stop here!" commanded Yakamura. "That will do." Then he turned around to Morgan, in the back seat, and said, "Get out of the car!"

Morgan complied at once. He got out of the Ford, slammed the door and then walked off, as if in deep thought, toward the freeway.

"Hey, hold it!" protested Webster. "That's not what I had in mind. I was given orders to—"

"Don't get excited!" Yakamura smiled gently. "You'll see in just a moment what I plan to do."

Yakamura looked at Vale. "Would you mind driving on a bit farther from the freeway and then turning around to go back where we came from?"

Vale shook his head and took off. Webster peered through the rear window, nonplussed by Morgan's strange actions. Morgan had set out on his way back to the main road without even once looking back at the car driving off in the opposite direction.

Vale continued on for another mile, then made a U-turn and drove back. In the meantime it had started raining.

Ten minutes later they spotted Morgan. Yakamura suggested, "Stop the car when you see him trying to hitch a ride!"

Morgan, in the meantime, had taken refuge from the rain under a tree by the wayside. He had pulled his jacket halfway over his head to protect himself from sudden downpour. He was frantically waving his thumb toward the freeway.

Vale braked and came to a full stop just in front of Morgan.

Morgan came running from under the protective tree and quickly opened the door. "Thank heavens!" he panted, and let himself fall into the seat next to the utterly amazed Webster. "I was out here trying to catch a thief and I thought I was hot on his trail, when that rainstorm came on all of a sudden. Would you please be so kind as to give me a ride back into town?"

The Japanese smiled obligingly at him. "Why, of course. Did you have any success with your chase?"

"No. I seem to have lost his trail when I came onto this side road here."

He continued with his story about a thief he had pursued. He rattled on and on, with the most minute details. Yakamura listened attentively, and Webster and Vale began to understand slowly with growing horror that Morgan had lost any memory of what had really happened to him.

And that was not all! Morgan had fabricated an artificial memory and would therefore never remember a Japanese by the name of Yakamura whose trail he had so hotly pursued.

Yakamura ordered Morgan to be let off at the outskirts of the city. Webster, who had finally got over his initial shock, started asking all kinds of questions.

But Yakamura did not answer. Instead he requested, "Stop at the nearest phone booth. I want to call AN 2-3551."

The preparations leading up to the arranged meeting gave it the character of a mysterious plot. Webster insisted that the Japanese should be blindfolded while he was being driven to the meeting place. Tako did not resist. He went along with their game.

He did not even endeavor to memorize the various bends

in the road. There was not the slightest doubt in his mind that these business negotiations would be concluded most successfully and that he would return unharmed.

He was most pleased that the Morgan affair had wound up so easily. How fortunate for him that chance had been on his side, saving him a lot of time consuming trouble.

At last they reached their destination, and the long walk through halls, up and down staircases and around corners came to an end.

The blindfold was removed from Tako's eyes. He found himself in a fairly well lit but not tastefully furnished room.

Several men standing around a large table looked him over curiously. They seemed to fit in with the style of the furniture.

"Good evening, gentlemen!" Tako said in the most friendly manner.

The men began to grin. "Good evening!" one of them replied. His face seemed familiar. His picture was frequently in the newspapers. Tako remembered the rumor that Stan Brabham's word meant more in the steelworkers' union than that of the big boss.

Tako was not very surprised by what he saw. He had expected something of the kind.

"Let's sit down here!" Brabham suggested cordially, and pulled over a chair for Tako.

"And let's start right away with business, Mr. Brabham," added Tako.

Brabham looked startled. "How come you know my name?"

"From the papers," replied Tako curtly. "Anyhow, what does it really matter? Let's come to the point—do you want to help me?"

Brabham answered with a brief nod.

"Why?" continued Tako.

"First of all because of the money and, more important still, because we sympathize with the Third Power."

Tako did not manage to hide his surprise. "Why? And how did you find out?"

"We have our people everywhere, and they know how to keep their eyes and ears open," explained Brabham with a wide grin. "We also have friends working at Ferroplastics,

Limited, for instance. To make a long story short, somebody got wind of the whole thing, and we were smart enough to figure out what it all added up to."

Tako looked straight into Brabham's eyes. "What will you be able to do for us?" he inquired.

Brabham was fiddling with a pencil stub and doodling on a piece of paper in front of him on the table. "We can get you about anything you want," he remarked calmly. "This is no exaggeration, either."

Tako fully believed him. He had heard about the tremendous influence wielded by the American trade unions.

"What will be your price?"

"Five percent gross," stated Brabham without blinking an eyelid.

That was quite a lot. Still, it was far less than Tako had expected to have to pay. "Why aren't you charging more for your services?"

"That's all we need," replied Brabham. "And besides, I have already told you how much we admire you. You have every chance to become a third world power indeed. We, the workers, don't want to be left out and wait passively when we see such a chance to bring about final peace on Earth."

"But do you realize that you are working against the laws of your own country?"

Brabham shrugged with deliberation. "This particular law is nonsense. Everyone will come to that conviction in a few more years."

Tako thought for a moment before he shot off his first question. "Can you get us some magnetic bottles with a volume of 1,000 cubic yards each?"

Brabham turned to the man next to him. "Jeff, how about it?"

"No problem," affirmed Jeff. "We'll get them for you."

Brabham turned again to Tako. "You have heard it yourself. How many magnetic bottles will you need?"

"Five."

"When?

"As soon as possible."

"Jeff, how long will it take you?"

"Four to five weeks."

"In five weeks, will that do?"

"Okay with us."

"Anything else you need?"

"That will be all for the time being, Mr. Brabham. I don't want to play all my cards before I have seen positive proof that you can really deliver what you promise. I hope you understand my being cautious."

Brabham laughed out loud and slapped his hand on the table. "I understand. But we will convince you that we mean business."

"I will leave it up to you how you go about seeing that no one finds out who placed the order," Tako said.

"Don't you worry," Brabham reassured him. "We are not interested in risking our own necks, either."

After discussing the terms of delivery, Tako left the meeting with shining eyes, very satisfied with what he had accomplished. Back at the hotel, he paid his bill, and he left Pittsburgh early the next morning.

CHAPTER FIVE

Rarely had Perry Rhodan felt such gratitude toward anyone as he did now for Khrest. For the Arkonide scientist had made sure not to be around when Rhodan regained consciousness after the hypnoschooling session.

Only Rhodan's friend Bell was present. As soon as Bell awoke he sat up and turned his back to Rhodan; then he leaned forward and supported his head in his hands, as if its weight had suddenly become more than he could bear.

An hour went by without a word being spoken. Rhodan stared inside his brain and saw an endless cave in which he could perceive everything clearly. In the cave was stored all types of information, innumerable items of specialized superior knowledge. All he needed to do was to formulate any wish in his mind, and instantaneously he would have the solution to it, if it was something of a mathematical or scientific nature.

He tried to estimate the extent of this cavern which was his brain. But he was incapable of perceiving any limit to it. It seemed infinite, and as far as he managed to peer into it, he never encountered any wall; there was always still another path leading farther on.

He looked up. His glance fell on the telecom. He felt absolutely convinced that Thora was observing him on the other end in her own cabin. She was surely studying his reaction upon awakening. He did not want to give her the satisfaction of seeing him brood over the newly found insights that the superior Arkonide treasure of knowledge was giving him.

He got up. Bell was annoyed and grumbled about the noise Rhodan was making. Perry walked along the corridor until he came to the open door leading into Khrest's room. Khrest was sitting in a jointed chair staring at the telecom screen in Thora's cabin.

Upon hearing Rhodan entering, Khrest turned his head. "Well?" he asked, and smiled with a trace of concern.

"Oh, nothing." Rhodan shook his head. "I have found a mistake."

Khrest straightened up with a shock. "A mistake?"

"Yes. The solution of the problem seems to be of a fairly recent date. I suppose that your people were too phlegmatic to look at everything properly."

Khrest appeared to wince. Rhodan winked an eye toward the telecom, to make Khrest understand that his words were really for Thora's ears.

"Very interesting, indeed!" whispered Khrest. "And what kind of mistake have you detected?"

"The problem of reproducing hyperflight routes—do you remember?" Rhodan asked as nonchalantly as he could. "The differential equation on which it is based is unstable and cannot be solved according to formula. The differential equation is one of the seventh order. But you were using a numerical approximation of the thirteenth order. That means that it is by several degrees more unstable than even the differential equation itself. In the field of nonstability small deviations grow to big mistakes.

"Even in our own mathematics here on Earth there are approximately solutions of the seventh order for such basic equations," continued Rhodan. "Shall I tell you why this mistake was made on Arkon?"

Khrest could say nothing in reply.

"The reason is that the approximation method used is conveniently easy to apply," roared Rhodan harshly, "and because these methods are made to order for your automatic calculating machines, as I have discovered from another source of information now stored in my brain. Your scientists' inertia made them neglect to examine the basic equation for its stability, and only that same inertia caused them to employ the usual procedure."

Rhodan's voice now assumed a severely sarcastic note. "And this same inertia permits a considerable number of mistakes in the result and as a consequence uses an immense amount of energy to reproduce a once used hyperflight route.

"Do you realize"—and now Rhodan's words came with the impact of repeated hammer blows—"that one-tenth of the calculated energy used would be sufficient!"

Rhodan felt pain as he observed how Khrest reacted. Khrest collapsed into his chair, sat bent over, muttering fragments of sentences, shaking his head in desperation.

Rhodan avoided looking at the telecom screen. He knew that Thora was observing him and could understand him. This farce was really intended for her benefit rather than for Khrest. The mistake did exist, but the way he had brought up the subject was aimed at her. Rhodan would have loved to be able to see her face.

Slowly Khrest regained his composure. Rhodan smiled at him reassuringly to help him regain his equilibrium.

"I really had not intended to discuss this mistake with you, Khrest. I came here to thank you for everything you have done for us. You can't imagine how much we are in your debt, how appreciative we are."

Khrest saw through Rhodan's attempt to cheer him up. He started to smile but managed only to produce a rather painful grimace. "Please don't, Rhodan," he murmured feebly, "You are not the one who should be grateful. It is just the other way around—we ourselves must thank the fate that let the paths of our two races cross."

Khrest leaned forward again. "Do you know that no one has ever dared to absorb the knowledge of ten levels of developmental steps at one time? Do you realize how long I had to observe you before I was sure you could risk this jump without endangering your mind?"

Khrest breathed deeply. Then he continued, "I had expected you would need several days to recover from the tremendous shock of the ten level schooling. And what do you do? You get off the couch, and hardly has the transmitter been disconnected before you come to me and tell me, 'This is where you fools made a mistake!' "

Khrest's voice grew loud and strong. "Do you realize what that means?"

Anyone could guess the answer. Khrest sank back again into his chair, breathing with effort.

The loud clatter of hurried steps became audible rushing down the corridor approaching Khrest's room. At the same time Rhodan could hear Bell mumbling something to himself. Now the stocky figure of Rhodan's redheaded friend appeared in the door.

"Listen, Perry!" he said earnestly. "They have made a mistake—you know that, don't you? When they tried to reproduce mathematically a hyperflight they applied a differential equation of the seventh order. And in addition . . ."

Rhodan burst out laughing, startling Khrest. It looked as if Rhodan's uncontrollable peals of laughter were painful for Khrest to bear. But then Khrest overcame his feelings of hurt and mustered a quiet, resigned smile and an occasional chuckle at the grotesque situation.

An hour later the vessel left its orbital spin around Earth and set course for the moon. Rhodan had taken over the guidance system, applying the newfound information he had obtained during the hypnoindoctrination.

Reginald Bell flew as co-pilot. Khrest sat in the background, staring straight ahead. From time to time Rhodan turned around to check up on him. It seemed odd how long it took for a person of such mental magnitude to find his emotional balance again.

Thora did not come to the command center until the vessel was already heading straight for the moon. Rhodan did not bother to turn around as she entered. He heard her say, "This ship has an automatic guidance system. You are wasting your time, Rhodan!"

It was intended to sound sarcastic, but she was furious to note how poorly she succeeded.

Bell had turned around. "We are familiar with the workings of the Arkonide automatic guidance systems," he countered calmly. "One of them made quite a mess of fighting off an attack by three hydrogen helium rockets from Earth—didn't it, Thora?"

Rhodan was unable to observe Thora's reaction to Bell's squelch. He noticed only utter silence on her part. When Bell turned around, facing front again, the corners of his mouth were twitching while he tried to suppress a loud chuckle.

They carried a large assortment of highly sensitive radiation counters on board. Rhodan hovered above the spot where they had located the remains of the former Arkonide cruiser while Bell carried out the necessary measurements for lingering radiation.

There had been no fallout on the moon. Whatever radioactivity had been generated by the bombs had either been shot straight out into space or remained on the ground. The lack of atmosphere at the same time lessened the danger for those who wanted to approach the site of the explosion.

Whatever remained of the cruiser did not reveal whether any part of the gigantic vehicle had escaped total destruction. Rhodan knew that there was hope for the innermost cell. Its walls had been constructed of a type of metal plastic. This material possessed a field of crystallization that imparted a degree of hardness and constancy of temperature beyond that known by terrestrial metallurgy. Any hull made of this metal plastic would stand up to unbelievable stress and would withstand temperatures up to 80,000 degrees Celsius.

The outside walls of the cruiser formed a chaotic tangle of molten and congealed material. Even if the innermost cell had remained undamaged, they would have to find a way through this confusion of highly radioactive plastic metal to get at the cell.

Bell announced, "Two microroentgens per hour!"

"At an altitude of fifty miles," completed Rhodan. "That means we will have to expect about fifty to a hundred roentgens per hour down at the origin of the radiation, considering the extent of the source."

Reginald Bell nodded. "That means we can't use our own protective suits."

Rhodan turned to Khrest. "This ship has protective clothing against high radiation on board, and we also carry a decontamination unit. There is no reason why we shouldn't land and inspect the wreck from nearby."

Khrest had no objections; he simply nodded agreement.

Rhodan landed the vessel about a mile from the outer limit of the area where the remnants of the former Arkonide cruiser lay scattered about.

"I want to go out there with Reg. Whatever has to be done must be carried out quickly; we are just the right people for such a job. Khrest, I want to make sure that we remain in constant radio communication. I don't want to run any more risks."

As an additional safeguard, Rhodan stepped over to the steering console, disconnected the motors that supplied the propulsion power and ran them down to zero output. That would guarantee a delay of at least half an hour if anyone suddenly decided to start them. He wanted to make sure Thora could not take off at lightning speed, leaving them stranded in this radioactive hell.

Khrest managed a faint smile of amusement. Thora did not move, but in her eyes the red pupils were scintillating with bright fury. Bell left the room to get the protective suits.

These were far more efficiently constructed than the suits Rhodan and his crew had used for their first moon landing with the *Stardust*. It had then taken them about twenty minutes to put on their protective space suits, a feat that, if properly executed with all required control measures, taxed their patience. They were pleased that they could simply slip on the Arkonide suits like ordinary coveralls. A little light came on at the left wrist indicating that everything was in order. There were no cumbersome oxygen tanks, no heavy radio in the helmet, no insulating bulges around the neck to interfere with free head movements and prevent them from throwing their heads back if they wanted to look upward. The Arkonide suit produced its own oxygen supply from chemicals that took up hardly any space and were of negligible weight. The miniature telecom took up less space than a fingernail. The helmet was part of the suit and did not require airtight fitting.

Rhodan and Bell armed themselves with needle ray beamers. It was most likely that the three exploded bombs had blocked off the access to the interior of the cruiser. The needle ray beamer developed a focal temperature of close to 90,000 degrees Fahrenheit. They would have to resort to more efficient but heavier instruments if none of the hatches of the inner cell could be opened easily.

Khrest gazed after the two Earthmen as they left the ship via one of its air locks. Thora paid no attention to them. She stood in front of a screen and stared at the wreckage of the formerly proud Arkonide research ship.

"Watch her!" Rhodan admonished the Arkonide scientist, and it did not matter to him at all whether Thora heard his words.

They switched on the generators and slowly penetrated the area of the explosion. The molten, formless pieces were a frightening sight at close range.

No word was exchanged between the two men. Only Khrest's voice could be heard from time to time: "Everything okay aboard ship."

Rhodan landed near the largest heap of wreckage he could find. It was most probable that it would contain the inner cell of the cruiser.

Bell moaned as he threw his head back to see the top of the mountain of rubble.

They began to work at once. The needle ray beamer cut the debris into big chunks and opened a passage for them. The dosimeter recorded ten roentgens, and they had been away from the ship barely ten minutes.

The only reassuring factor was Khrest's repeated reports: "Everything okay aboard ship."

An hour later they had advanced about twenty yards inside the rubble heap.

Rhodan worried that the structure would not be sufficiently stable to tolerate a twenty yard wide hole in its interior. He asked Bell to stop working for a while and proceeded to knock at the surrounding material. He left his hand resting on the spot for a moment to watch for any unusual reactions. But he could not detect anything besides the vibrations that were to be expected from the metal plastic.

Rhodan motioned to Bell to resume the work. In another hour they were really making headway. They reached large fissures and gaps inside the wreckage and could advance large stretches without having to use the needle ray beamer.

"We have penetrated almost fifty yards," murmured Bell. "We should have reached it by now."

"Maybe we are already inside it!" ventured Rhodan.

Bell turned around abruptly.

Rhodan nodded. "We have no guarantee that the inner cell was able to withstand the bombing attack. The crystal field might have failed."

Bell was breathing hard. "Well, then . . . !" he snorted, and pointed the beam against the nearest obstacle in their way.

A moment later he shouted triumphantly, "Look here, Perry! We've made it!"

Rhodan peered over his shoulder. The last piece of metal plastic had been detached from an expanse of smooth wall. This wall had not been affected by the heat of the explosion; they could see this right away.

Rhodan knew that metal plastic crystal reinforcement was turquoise blue, the same as the wall Bell had uncovered.

They resumed their endeavors with renewed strength and managed to expose large parts of the wall. Khrest began to put questions to them, but they answered him only briefly.

"This seems to be a door!" Bell panted finally.

He had found the small indentation in the wall. The line ran diagonally, a sign that the inner cell had changed position because of the explosion. It took another fifteen minutes for them to uncover the door completely. Rhodan knew that the door had been automatically sealed the instant the explosion occurred. He would need to find the special code that would unlock it again, provided the opening mechanism was still in working order.

He pulled out the impulse set that he had brought along from the Arkonide vessel. It was a pencil-like rod about four inches long that contained a code sender; he pressed it against the door.

Suddenly he felt the ground tremble beneath him. The door seemed to strain, as if it wanted to open. There were heaving and squeaking in the door joints, but only a hair-breadth wide chink became visible. Then it closed again, unable to overcome the forces pulling against it.

Rhodan motioned to Bell. The door was about man size and not too heavily built. Human muscle power would supply the additional push needed to open it completely.

Once more Rhodan applied the impulse set; once again the ground began to vibrate and a tiny gap showed itself along the edge of the door. This time the opening was a bit wider, just big enough so that Bell could insert his gloved fingertips and get a firm grip on it.

He leaned heavily against the door frame, all the while pulling at the door with all his might. Rhodan kept the impulse set constantly pressed against the turquoise plastic metal of the door slab.

Bell changed his position and renewed his efforts. The obstacle gave way so suddenly that Bell was thrown violently back against the wall of the corridor. The fully opened door revealed a darkened closet size air lock.

Khrest's voice came over the radio. "Everything okay here. How is it going with you?"

"We are facing a difficult decision," replied Rhodan. "The door is finally open. The air lock seems to be in fine working order. We had a hard time prying the entrance open. If we enter now in the regular manner, we might risk not being able to open the door again from the inside when we want to leave."

"Well, what is your problem then?" inquired Khrest.

"I can open the other end of the air lock without first

closing the door leading to the outside. But then the air inside the inner cell would rush out with explosive force."

"Would that endanger you?" asked Khrest. "Can't you take cover in time?"

"We can take care of ourselves; we are perfectly safe here," said Rhodan. "But how about any possible survivors inside the cell? How about their chances of living through that?"

Khrest's heavy breathing became quite audible. "This seems most improbable. If anybody had lived through the atomic bombing, he would long since have found a way to establish communication with us."

"What if he was seriously wounded and could not move at all?"

Khrest sighed deeply. Then he spoke up calmly. "Just go ahead and open the inside door of the air lock. We can't afford to take any more chances now. We desperately need the objects inside the cell. We must get them immediately!"

Rhodan nodded, approving Khrest's decision. He would not have chosen a different solution, but in moments like these it seemed better to share responsibility.

Reginald Bell took the impulse set from Rhodan and walked over to the other end of the air lock. "Here is a good spot where I can take cover. Perry, stay outside!"

The door to the interior functioned perfectly. As it opened a rush of air escaped, accompanied by a cloud of dust and a few small objects that had not been fastened down. The heavy air wave lasted but a second. Then the atmosphere had completely vanished.

As Rhodan entered the air lock, Bell jumped up from behind his shelter. "Good grief!" he moaned. "That felt as if somebody hit me over the head with a sandbag."

Rhodan peered inside the cell. It was pitch dark. He switched on the searchlight on his helmet and lit up the way leading to the interior of the cell. He noticed that the interior had been much more severely damaged by the force of the explosion than had the outside hull. The pressure had turned everything upside-down and even torn heavy instruments from their positions.

Many items had been destroyed or damaged beyond repair. But quite a few things could still be used. They would save themselves a lot of trouble if they brought everything back to Earth with them.

Bell was eagerly investigating this treasure trove. Just as Rhodan was about to call out to his friend, Khrest's excited voice came over the radio. "Emergency! Rhodan, Bell! Return at once!"

Rhodan stopped. "What's happened?"

"Hurry back as fast as you can! Don't lose a moment!" urged Khrest.

Rhodan whirled and took off. Bell followed. They switched off the artificial gravity and pushed out through the sinuous corridor they had blasted for themselves a short time ago.

Once outside, they set their generators for countervalues and sailed in a high arc over the Arkonide ship. Khrest had already opened the air lock for them. They lost precious seconds while the air lock was pumped full of air.

Khrest received them directly behind the inner door to the air lock. He was trembling, and his eyes shone red.

"What's the matter?" inquired Rhodan abruptly.

"Something terrible has happened," whispered Khrest.

Rhodan ran toward the command center. Khrest could hardly keep up with him.

"Thora has activated a hyperprobe. This was not against our agreements, and I did not prevent her from doing it."

Rhodan nodded briefly, removing his space suit while still hurrying to get to the command center. Hyperprobes were intended to locate the directional beam of a hypersender. The beam could be aimed to a fraction of an inch, and wherever it did not hit directly, it was unnoticeable. However, there were fully automatic probes, small vessels the size of a man's hand, that could search a certain area inch by inch and find any hyperdirectional beam that might be present.

Rhodan and Khrest reached the command center. Thora was standing leaning against the control panel, her face turned toward them. Rhodan recognized the mixture of pride and sarcasm in her expression.

Rhodan wasted only a brief glance at her.

Khrest continued his report, his voice quivering with

excitement. "The probe searched for some time outside without any success. But suddenly it did locate something."

"What did it locate?" Rhodan urged impatiently.

"The impulses of our own hypersender . . ." Khrest motioned quickly over to the picture screen that showed the image of the destroyed cruiser. "Coming from our wrecked spaceship over there. Automatic emergency signals. Do you know what that means?"

Rhodan understood at once. More than that, he also understood the consequences. Each Arkonide spaceship was equipped with a hypersender whose capacity was of the same structure, seen mathematically, as that of the hypergravitational field that made possible the faster than light flight through the universe. Hyperwaves traveled with barely any loss of time across any distance and therefore represented the ideal means of communication in an era that calculated in light-years with the same matter of fact attitude as earthlings had done with miles until recently.

Every hypsersender had an emergency switch that was activated as soon as anything happened to the spaceship carrier, regardless of whether it was caused by outside interference or mechanical failure inside the ship. Once set in motion the sender broadcast a certain signal uninterruptedly. Furthermore, it compressed the beam and directed it toward the next receiving station.

Rhodan was informed that the receiver to which the emergency signal was beamed from the destroyed cruiser was on Myra IV. He knew that Myra IV was nothing but a cold deserted planet in the vicinity of a dying sun, about 800 light-years from here. This planet was so inhospitable that the Empire had stationed there only the usual outpost detachment of robot ships.

The consequences could be easily foreseen. The robot ships would receive the emergency signals, then set out to approach the sender. They would determine that the cruiser had been destroyed by rockets, and they would then proceed to locate the spot where these missiles had originated and take revenge on the perpetrators of the attack.

In this case the perpetrators were Earthlings, and therefore they, as well as all other inhabitants of Earth, would be annihilated, together with their planet. There was no doubt that it was in the power of the robot ships to mete out full punishment to the offender.

The hypersender of the wrecked Arkonide exploratory vessel on the moon was sending out the emergency signals. This meant simply that within forty-five days after the destruction of the ship, someone would try to turn Earth into a rubble heap. And the way things looked now, Earth would not be able to fend off this attempt.

The only people who could help Earth in its plight were not at all in accord.

Rhodan glanced over at Khrest. Khrest seemed to guess his thoughts.

"I have started the motors already," he said.

Rhodan was relieved and thankful. "Let's start as quickly as possible, then."

CHAPTER SIX

Umanak Fjord, David Strait.

This is, according to anyone who has ever been there, where it is impossible to distinguish the gray sky from the equally gray icebergs.

There hardly exists a more disconsolate place on Earth. On the other hand, nowhere else on Earth are such important decisions made.

Umanak Fjord is headquarters of the International Intelligence Agency, which for the time being was just as overrun by foreign agents as by those of the IIA.

Very little was to be seen above ground. A few thick walled wooden houses belonging to a Danish trading firm were lived in by some Eskimos. On one of the houses a primitive wooden board nailed above the front door said in crooked painted letters that furs were sold in this establishment. But no one had ever purchased any furs from the Umanak Fur Co.

The Eskimos were well trained special agents. The manager of the post was a Dane. In reality he held the rank of first lieutenant and was Allan D. Mercant's special pet.

The rest of the installation was hidden under ice and rock. More than ninety-five percent of all activities at Umanak Fjord were carried on underground.

About 500 people lived permanently at Umanak Fjord. Only ten of those were familiar with the extent of the underground installations. The agents of the Asiatic Federation and of the Eastern Bloc who lived here during these days of enforced cooperation knew only the two upper stories.

Colonel Mercant's living and working quarters were on the lowest level of the tract. He was surrounded by security guards and safety installations. Not that he was afraid for his own personal safety. What mattered to him and to those responsible for these precautionary measures was the tremendous number of valuable and secret documents stored in safes built into the lowest floor.

Mercant worked in his private office, which he had furnished according to his own taste. The furniture was outsized. Any visitor had to look around this office and its gigantic furnishings to locate the colonel. Mercant as a rule sat behind a giant writing desk, comfortably leaning back in an armchair that was far too big for his slender figure. His head was hardly visible above the edge of his desk.

Mercant did not adhere to any fixed schedule. He worked until he got tired and felt that his efficiency was not up to par. Then he went to bed and slept until he felt sufficiently rested to carry on his work, The even illumination of his rooms enabled him to abandon the normal twenty-four hour rhythm of the world above.

The only ones to suffer from such an unorthodox time schedule were Mercant's orderlies. Most of them loved well ordered activity and well regulated hours for rest. But according to Mercant's point of view, world security should not be neglected because of subaltern officers' preference for well regulated working hours.

That day he had risen at 3 o'clock, not bothering whether it was 3 in the morning or in the afternoon. He had started to work on some papers that he had been forced to lay aside before he had gone to bed.

At 3:15 sharp Sergeant O'Healy had appeared and announced, "Nothing special has happened, sir, during the past four hours."

Then he had left the room, to return a few minutes later with some coffee and cookies. He waited patiently until Mercant had swallowed a few gulps of the boiling hot beverage and asked him the usual question: "What is the time now, Sergeant?"

"Three twenty-three, sir."

Mercant peered over the rim of his coffee cup and looked at the clock on the opposite wall. It showed 3:22.

"Which time of the day?"

"In the morning, sir."

Mercant smiled with satisfaction. Then O'Healy saluted and left the room. He no longer pondered about the odd ceremony, although he had considered it a silly joke when he first started working for Mercant.

Medical cosmetics were capable of a few tricks that were quite difficult to detect. Therefore, to protect himself against any eventualities, Mercant had ordered his sergeant on guard always to tell the time one minute faster than it really was. Also he had to say that it was morning when it was really evening and vice versa.

O'Healy was convinced that Mercant would shoot him on the spot if he ever told him the right time by mistake.

But he was wrong to assume that. Mercant considered it sufficient identification when O'Healy announced the time one minute too fast. However, the announcement of the time of day was a source of genuine information for him. Not until O'Healy told him that it was morning did he know that it was indeed afternoon.

Half an hour later he received Captain Zimmerman, who came to give his daily report.

"To begin with the most important bit of news—the interview with the officers of the Asiatic Federation. Major Perwuchin from Moscow arrived as an observer."

"What does he intend to observe?" inquired Mercant in a bored voice. "Do you have any idea what these Orientals want from us now?"

"Rumor has it that they have brought along many new proposals that they would like to discuss with you, sir."

"What kind of proposals? For a lasting world peace?"

"No, sir. Proposals on how they could get at those deserters in the Gobi Desert."

Mercant raised his right hand and carefully inspected his fingernails. "Don't keep on calling these people 'deserters,' Zimmerman! I have heard a great many good reports about them, and I would not like to judge them before I have learned what their motivations are."

Zimmerman did not reply.

"Anything else?" asked Mercant.

"Nothing else for the time being, sir."

"Thank you."

Zimmerman saluted and left the room.

Rhodan made a landing 180 miles inland on a smooth expanse of gray blue ice. The icy plain was of limited size and was surrounded on all sides by mountains of considerable height. There was no danger that the spacecraft might be discovered accidentally. Besides, 180 miles was quite a considerable distance for conditions on Greenland.

Thanks to the technical aids he had on board, Rhodan had experienced no particular difficulties in eluding the numerous radar stations in the area. He was certain that the observers had not even noted a slight flash on their radar screens.

Rhodan had not been worried at all about being detected by direct optical observation. The visibility ceiling was extremely low over Greenland, and it was easier to remain above the uninterrupted cloud cover than to surround the whole craft with an energy consuming deflector screen.

While flying back from the moon, Rhodan had informed Tako of all that had happened and had requested him to return to the Gobi Desert Base. Right now there were more important matters to deal with than to try to negotiate with the mighty captains of industry. Rhodan was justifiably convinced that the Third Power would soon no longer be forced to place its orders secretly, constantly afraid of detection by hostile agents.

Rhodan left the Arkonide spaceship in the afternoon. He was armed with a needle ray beamer and dressed in an Arkonide transporter suit. Bell remained aboard ship, since Thora's rebellious attitude had entered a new active phase following the discovery they had made on the moon. Khrest was no match for her—she needed more efficient surveillance.

With the help of the Arkonide transporter suit Rhodan could cover the 180 miles to Umanak Fjord within an hour and a half. The flight was uninteresting and tedious. In addition, Rhodan was plagued by feelings of uncertainty about the situation he would have to face in Umanak Fjord.

The only indication Rhodan had regarding Mercant's friendly attitude toward the Third Power was Lieutenant Klein's statement that Mercant was aware of the double role Klein was playing and that Mercant seemed to approve of it.

Rhodan used the deflector the moment he left the spaceship. The deflector field obtained energy from a microgenerator in the transporter suit. This field controlled electromagnetic radiation on all wavelengths between 2,000 and 8,000 angstroms and forced the waves to flow around the transporter suit like water around a rock. This meant that the wearer of such a suit could not be seen by the naked eye, by ultraviolet light or by infrared light. The suit was powerless against detection by radar, but on the other hand, the wearer of the suit presented too small a target to be picked up on a radar screen.

Rhodan landed right in the middle of the Umanak Fur Co., still not sure where he would have to go to find Mr. Mercant. The only thing he knew was that Mercant was somewhere below the surface of the earth. Rhodan's first task, therefore, was to find the entrance to the subterranean structure.

Even wearing a cloak of invisibility presented its problems to Rhodan, trying to avoid discovery by people. Umanak Fjord was as busy as a beehive. When two persons approached Rhodan from two different directions, he had to use a great deal of concentration to get out of their way.

Toward 4 o'clock in the afternoon Rhodan believed he had found the spot where the underground installations could be entered. From the outside nothing could be noticed, just a few low storage sheds. Rhodan had been standing nearby and observed a number of people that disappeared into the building or emerged from it.

Rhodan walked over to the door and waited nearby until the next man went in. Rhodan slid inside with him and entered the big hall. The interior was illuminated by arc lights, and the opposite wall showed the opening of a tall, wide shaft.

The heavy traffic in this shaft represented quite a danger for Rhodan. While passing down the next fifty yards from the entrance to the elevators, he was incapable of paying attention to anything but watching out that nobody bumped into him.

There were fifteen elevators. Rhodan did not dare to use one alone. He waited until a man entered an elevator, and then he quickly slipped inside.

Unfortunately for Perry Rhodan, that man descended only two floors. Rhodan remained alone in the elevator. A uniformed guard stuck his head inside the cabin.

"Okay," mumbled the guard. "Ready to go."

The moment his attention was diverted, Rhodan pushed the button for the lowest floor. The elevator started to move down swiftly.

As soon as the elevator had stopped, Rhodan left it. A tunnel stretched out to either side, looking similar to the shaft above. A lit up number *15* was visible on the wall opposite the elevator entrance. Rhodan had been counting as he descended. This, then, was the fifteenth floor below the ground.

Several guards were stationed below the lit up *15*. Two of them walked over to the elevator from which Rhodan had just alighted. One of the guards inspected the empty cabin and called out to his colleagues, "Hey! What do you know! Somebody pushed fifteen from the inside, but there isn't anybody. Where did he go?"

Two of his friends approached, and they in turn searched the empty elevator. They seemed to be quite puzzled, and one of them marched down the corridor toward a telephone. Rhodan had to jump aside to prevent the man from running into him. The man began to make his call, but Rhodan could not understand what he was saying.

Rhodan cursed himself. He should have known better! He should have remembered, from his days at Nevada Fields, this special type of elevator that indicated outside whether it had been set in motion from inside or outside. He should have guessed that Mercant would have this kind of elevator installed in his secret hideout.

The man left the phone, returned to the other guards still busy at the cabin and called out to them, "Stop the elevator! At once! Zimmerman wants to have a look at it!"

One of the men pushed the STOP button, and they stepped aside to await Zimmerman's arrival.

O'Healy reported, "An unexplained incident on the fifteenth floor, sir. Somebody took the elevator down to the fifteenth, but when the guard inspected the inside it was empty."

Mercant looked up. "Well, there was nobody inside. What does Zimmerman have to say to this?"

"Captain Zimmerman has called in some experts who are examining the interior of the elevator for fingerprints and such."

Mercant rose, sighing. "It will take them about three months to establish everyone who has left fingerprints in that elevator! Where did you say? On the fifteenth floor?"

"Yes, sir."

"Come along with me! We'll go up there."

In the meantime Rhodan had found out that the fifteenth floor was not the lowest. He went toward Captain Zimmerman, as the captain walked through the tunnel, and tried to determine where the captain had come from. This way Rhodan found the two elevator shafts that led farther down still but not up.

These elevators were even more closely guarded than the one he had taken down from the surface. There was no doubt that the guards would react immediately at the slightest movement of either elevator.

Rhodan waited. A little while later Zimmerman returned

from the other end of the tunnel with one of the sergeants. The guard saluted, and Zimmerman entered the elevator with the sergeant.

Rhodan jumped into the elevator, close behind the two. He avoided any noise and pushed himself flat against the cabin wall to avoid touching his two co-riders.

Zimmerman seemed puzzled. "That's strange. I am almost led to believe that the man must have leaped out of the moving elevator. But that's impossible!"

Suddenly the elevator came to a halt. Rhodan had been counting the floors and realized that they had descended another six floors.

Because he was afraid his shoes would clatter on the uncarpeted floor of the tunnel, Rhodan failed to jump out fast enough. The sergeant brushed past him and bumped into him.

The sergeant stopped in his tracks, which caused Zimmerman to collide with him. Rhodan held his breath and tiptoed to the side with tiny steps.

"What's the matter?" asked Zimmerman.

"I . . . I ran into something just now, sir."

Zimmerman frowned. "Where?"

"Right here, sir!" stammered the sergeant, and pointed into the air.

Rhodan saw that they were at the end of a corridor. The narrow side of the wall was two yards to the left of the wall. The two guards who had been standing across from the elevator exit approached.

Zimmerman laughed. "How long have you been working here with us, Sergeant?"

"Two years, sir."

Zimmerman nodded understandingly. "That explains it. When I was stationed here for two years, I began seeing little green men marching through the halls."

Zimmerman shoved his hands fairly close together to demonstrate how small these men had been. He seemed to want to cheer up the sergeant. "With all this secrecy," he added kindly, "it is no wonder if you get hallucinations after some time."

The sergeant pulled himself together. "Yes, sir!"

Rhodan was relieved. Zimmerman walked down the corridor with the sergeant, while the guards stayed behind, still grinning. Cautiously Rhodan walked past them and followed the two men down the hall.

"Here comes Zimmerman, sir!" announced O'Healy, as he opened one of the steel doors in front of Mercant. These steel doors divided the lowest tunnel into several sections.

Zimmerman saluted smartly. "This is Sergeant Daniels, sir. He was the first one to notice the incident."

Mercant turned to the sergeant. "You have ordered the whole elevator cabin searched for fingerprints?"

"Yes, sir. Not the whole cabin, though, only the push-button for the fifteenth floor."

"Very clever, very clever indeed," came Mercant's sarcastic reply. "That will keep a lot of your specialists happy for some time."

Zimmerman squirmed uncomfortably. "I have—"

"Doesn't it occur to you, Captain, that this man—if such a person really exists—might have employed the time honored device of wearing gloves? He seems to be an ingenious guy to begin with if he managed to penetrate the Umanak station. Don't you agree?"

"Yes, sir, that sounds reasonable," admitted Zimmerman meekly.

"You bet your life it does!" snapped Mercant. "Who besides yourself has seen that empty elevator?"

"All the guard posts stationed in front of the fifteenth floor elevator exit, sir," reported Daniels.

"Did you send for the repairman to check the elevators out for some failure of the electronic system, Zimmerman?" inquired Mercant.

"Not yet, sir. But I will see to it at—"

Before Zimmerman had a chance to complete his sentence he was interrupted by a sudden shrill whining sound. All hell seemed to break loose. The ear piercing noise drowned out all other sounds. The steel door near which Mercant was standing was set in motion automatically, knocking Mercant toward the back part of the tunnel. Mercant seized O'Healy's arm in time and pulled him back with him behind the closing door. Zimmerman and Daniels were left on the other side.

"Radar alarm!" shouted Mercant breathlessly. "Come on, O'Healy!"

They turned about-face and stormed down the corridor. They could not get to Mercant's private office, since the steel doors could be opened only by special order in such an emergency. Mercant did not want to issue this order as long as he did not know exactly what had happened. Therefore, he went into one of the offices in this section of the shaft.

He sat down at one of the writing desks and called the security center via intercom. "Mercant speaking. What's the matter with the bottom tunnel?"

"Radar alarm in Sector A, sir."

"What caused this alarm?"

"We don't know, sir. We've been scanning the whole sector, but nothing can be seen on the screen."

"Have you got in touch with the A Sector offices?"

"Yes, sir. We did this right away. But they haven't noticed anything unusual."

Mercant was thinking hard. Sector A was the first a person had to pass through coming from the elevators. If someone came down from above he had to get through that way.

"Give the all clear," Mercant said simply.

They could hear another siren howling outside in the corridors. Mercant called to O'Healy to follow him back to the door where he had been talking a couple of minutes ago with Zimmerman.

Zimmerman and Daniels were still rooted to the same spot as before.

"Have you noticed anything here; did you see anyone?" Mercant asked the two.

"No, sir. Nothing whatsoever. May I ask what—"

"Probably a ghost making its rounds," answered Mercant with a smile. "Or an invisible man, at least."

With cautious steps he walked past the two men farther down the hall. Zimmerman and the two sergeants were about to follow him, when Mercant waved them back. One of the doors on the left side of the corridor opened. A man stuck his head through the door, but Mercant angrily motioned him back into the room.

Suddenly Mercant came to a halt and drew himself up, as if he had found something. He peered down at the floor, then up again into the air; finally he turned around and came back smiling.

"There is nothing here. I can't find a thing. Enough of this tomfoolery!" Mercant said with amusement. "Zimmerman! Send those fingerprint experts home again. I believe we will be able to solve this mystery all by ourselves."

Mercant looked over to see the two sergeants. "O'Healy and Daniels, get back to your jobs. O'Healy, I will expect you to report to me at the usual time."

Then Mercant marched back to his office without bothering about the perplexed faces that stared after his disappearing figure. Cautiously he opened the door to his private office. A grin of satisfaction covered his features. He went to his desk, fell back into his armchair and pulled out a drawer, from which he took a gun.

Then he pointed the weapon at a spot between the door and the first filing cabinet. "Whoever you are," he said to the void, "you may remove your cloak of invisibility now. I don't know what you have in mind. But if you should intend finishing off old Mercant, I assure you that I still have enough strength to pull this trigger. I know exactly where you are standing, as you see. Well?"

A few seconds went by. Then a cloud formed right at the spot Mercant was aiming at. The cloud began to take shape and solidified into a man dressed in a strange looking suit.

Mercant's eyes grew wide with astonishment. "Major Rhodan!"

Perry Rhodan shook his head. "Address me only as Rhodan. The major has quit the service."

Now it was Rhodan's turn to express amazement. "How on Earth did you guess that I was hidden in this room?"

Mercant smiled. "People are saying about me that I can smell the presence of a person in a dark room. I have never experienced it as distinctly, though, as just now. Have a seat, please, Rhodan!"

Rhodan sat down. He seemed free and easy.

"Your outfit is ineffective against radar detection, it seems," Mercant stated calmly after a while.

"Yes. And I didn't know that you had a radar warning system down here."

"It was nevertheless a remarkable accomplishment, Rhodan!"

Rhodan shrugged. "Let's come to the point. It's quite serious, Mercant."

"All right! Shoot!"

Rhodan reported what had happened on the moon recently. He concluded, "I want to make this quite clear—we must expect the arrival of a number of robot ships in the near future. They will not ask if we were justified in destroying the Arkonide cruiser. They will simply attack us, and we will be defenseless."

Mercant did not indicate whether he was impressed by the report. He asked quietly, "Your auxiliary spaceship—didn't you say that it was well equipped? Can't you ward off the imminent attack with it?"

"Well equipped compared with what we humans have at our disposal, Mercant! But any means of defense we have will be no match for the approaching robot ships. We will do whatever is in our power, but the world, too, must get ready for the attack."

"How do I know that you aren't simply trying to bluff me in order to take unfair advantage of us?" countered Mercant.

"You don't know, and nobody can tell you," Rhodan said coldly. "You either believe me or not. You will find out in time that I am not bluffing you."

Mercant looked unimpressed; he seemed to reflect over what he just had heard. In reality he was trying to probe Rhodan's brain. Mercant was well aware that he had the beginnings of telepathic abilities. He was capable of perceiving thoughts if the person was concentrating on them and if that person was not too far away from him. In most cases, though, he could perceive only the total concept and the gestalt of certain ideas. And he knew intuitively whether that thought was the truth.

Rhodan's brain was different. Mercant had been able to locate Rhodan by sensing the presence of his brain. This is how he had pinpointed Rhodan's position from outside in the hall and then inside the office. But Mercant could not penetrate into Rhodan's brain at all. It was as if he had put a solid barrier around his thoughts. Although Mercant could not grasp any of his visitor's thoughts directly, he nevertheless sensed that his intentions were honest.

He stood up. "Let's forget the thing about the bluff, Rhodan," he said finally. "What would you suggest we do?"

"Make sure that the right people are informed about what we will have to expect soon. Describe it to them as vividly as you can and then explain that a proper defense system can be created only if everyone will cooperate with each other."

Rhodan's voice grew more intense. "In addition to that, will you see to it that this ridiculous embargo against our supply line with raw materials or any other products we need to buy is lifted. Even if we succeed in fighting off the first attack, others will certainly follow. In order to be in a good defensive position, we must make sure of having at least *one* effective spaceship at our disposal. Even if the industries should get permission to supply us with whatever we need, it will take us several months to construct the ship from the raw materials and the half-finished parts. But in case we have to procure all these things underground, we could do it only within a year or two!"

Mercant kept his eyes fixed on a spot on the floor. "I'll try to do my best, Rhodan. Do you realize what you are asking me to do? I'll fly to Washington and tell the people there, 'Listen, Rhodan has found a hypersender on the moon, a hypersender that is emitting automatic emergency signals. In two weeks at the most a fleet of robot ships will arrive and bombard our planet. Rhodan wants you to lift the embargo against his lines of supply.' What do you think the people will answer me?"

Rhodan mobilized all his reserve powers. "You are capable of exerting a tremendous influence on people, Mercant," he said softly but intensely, while locking his eyes with those of Mercant. "You will use this influence and persuade the people of the absolute necessity of avoiding any delay in the defensive measures that you will initiate against the impending attack from outer space. Is that clear, Mercant? Go directly to the President of the United States! Talk with those persons who believe you personally, not just because you are the chief of the IIA. Is that clear, Mercant?"

Mercant nodded obediently. It did not occur to him that never before had anyone dared talk to him in such a manner. It could not occur to him for the simple reason that Rhodan's command had been given in form of a hypnotic message. Mercant was compelled to carry it out exactly the way he had been ordered to.

Rhodan relaxed his grip on Mercant's mind. "I would appreciate if you would escort me safely back to the surface."

Mercant opened the door. "As long as you are with me no one will dare stop you."

While they were walking along the corridor Mercant remarked, "I will have to remain in touch with you, Rhodan. Inform Lieutenant Klein that he will receive any news for you by ANP code. Will you remember that?"

Rhodan stopped. Mercant was amused to notice his surprise.

"Who did you say should I inform about the ANP code?" replied Rhodan. "Klein? Lieutenant Klein?"

"That's right."

"How did you know that he was working with us?"

"I did not know it for sure," said Mercant. "I simply presumed he did. Didn't I tell you that my sense of intuition is developed to an extraordinary degree? I can 'smell' certain things."

Rhodan recovered from his surprise. "Klein will be most pleased to learn about this. He was in constant fear of being found out by someone who would not approve of what he was doing."

Mercant began to chuckle. "Never mind that. I still consider him one of my best agents!"

They reached the elevators, where the amazed guards gave a smart salute to their superior Mercant and his strange looking companion.

"How would you explain your attitude toward Klein, Mercant?" Rhodan asked.

Mercant hesitated before he replied straightforwardly, "It is my belief that mankind should collaborate with you. I am convinced that you intend no evil for the human race and that it would be to our advantage to make our peace with you."

Rhodan looked up at Mercant, his eyes filled with astonishment. He stretched out his hand to Mercant.

"Thank you, my friend."

CHAPTER SEVEN

Allan D. Mercant was one of the few people the President would receive at any time.

Both men wielded power and influence in a comparable manner, the only difference being that the President was officially authorized to do what Mercant accomplished under the mantle of secrecy. But in this particular case Mercant depended on the President's assistance—only he was empowered to give the signal for an atomic alarm.

President Nyson had invited a special adviser to be present at the interview. Next to Mercant, Mr. Wildinger was considered one of the most lucid minds in the world.

Mercant had not been able to persuade the President.

President Nyson protested, "No one could possibly demand that I should act on a mere rumor and release the atomic alarm and start spending money wildly. Do you realize, Mercant, that such an alarm would cost about a billion dollars?"

Mercant remained unruffled. "I can't imagine why this should matter to us in such an emergency."

President Nyson reacted impatiently. "Wildinger! What are you waiting for! Let's hear your opinion!"

Wildinger had been listening to the discussion, comfortably settled in his big armchair. Now he leaned forward. "This is a rather ticklish affair," he began. "We might decide to economize and not spend the billion dollars but lose our lives a few days later because of it. On the other hand, it might turn out all right if we don't proceed with the atomic alarm. After all, we have heard nothing but suspicions from Mr. Mercant, no concrete facts. Unless Mercant can supply us with all the information he is basing his report on, nothing can be assumed as certainty."

Wildinger lit a cigarette and continued, "I am in favor of a compromise. Let's prepare for the eventuality of an impending alarm, so that we will be able to act immediately if necessary. That will cost only one-tenth of what a real alarm would come to."

Mercant breathed a secret sigh of relief. This was exactly what he had hoped to accomplish. He had insisted on calling a state of emergency, with full atomic alarm, but he knew he would have to settle for a state of alert.

Nyson gave his consent to Wildinger's proposal, and Mercant did so with apparent reluctance. He rose from the conference table, concluding with a soft voice, "I'll inform the other parties about that. I wouldn't want them to believe that we are secretly preparing for a hostile confrontation with them."

The other parties Mercant referred to were the two power blocs centered in Moscow and Peking. Nyson had no objections to Mercant's suggestion.

In Moscow and Peking, Mercant's report of the impending attack from outer space was received with the same attitude of disbelief as it had been in Washington. But disbelief soon gave way to amazement and fear. According to the reports from the secret agents that Moscow and Peking had stationed in Washington, the Western world was indeed preparing for the possibility of an atomic alarm.

To maintain the delicate balance of power, the two big powers were forced to initiate the same state of atomic preparedness. They did so without really knowing the score.

The population of the three power blocs remained ignorant of what was going on behind the scenes. As a result an atmosphere of calm and peace reigned over the world.

The Arkonide vessel returned to the base in the Gobi Desert. The robots were busy completing their tasks.

Tako had come back the previous day and brought along

the news of the hypersender that was just about to bring havoc to Earth. Manoli and Haggard, the two physicians who had remained behind on the Third Power territory, had been cut off from direct communication with Rhodan and his group during their recent expedition to the moon. The doctors had almost reached their mental breaking point by the time the spacecraft with Rhodan landed near the *Stardust I.*

Rhodan called his friends Manoli and Haggard and told them in detail about everything that had happened in the meantime. Both physicians, who did not possess the remarkable knowledge of Rhodan and Bell, reacted to the news of the threatening danger with great shock.

A briefing session followed for all the members of the Third Power. Manoli and the Australian participated in it, but they were depressed and silent.

Thora was just as silent but not at all depressed. Her face still showed an expression of triumph. Rhodan could understand her feelings. She saw the day approaching when she would no longer have to depend on these Earthlings she so despised. She planned to ascend in her Arkonide spaceship to evade the attacking robot spacecraft. They would identify her auxiliary vessel as the last useful remainder of the destroyed Arkonide cruiser and would take it aboard their own robot ship. Then they would transport her and Khrest back to their home planet, Arkon.

Rhodan opened the meeting with the words "There is no doubt in our minds that we can neither change nor influence the plans of the approaching robot spaceships. That means that we cannot prevent them from attacking Earth. Once these robots start out, in response to an emergency signal that was sent as a result of an enemy attack, the enemy can do nothing to escape the robots' punitive measures.

"Therefore, it is no use even to think about finding a way to escape from the robots' mission of vengeance. The only other solution would be to work out a plan to attack and destroy the robots before they even get near our world, which they intend to change into a rubble heap."

The question had been thrown out. The only ones even capable of making effective considerations of the problem were Thora, Khrest, Bell and Rhodan. Tako, Manoli and Haggard did not possess the necessary intellectual prerequisites. But of the four who did, Thora preferred to remain silent. Khrest was so overwhelmed by the apparent hopelessness of the situation that he could not judge rationally. His superior mental faculties were rendered inefficient by his emotional attitude of defeat. The only two capable of remaining lucid in face of the seemingly insurmountable odds were Bell and Rhodan.

"Let's look at this matter from a tactical point of view," suggested Bell. "According to the emergency signal code we must count on being attacked by five robot ships. The only question is, what will the reactions of these ships be?

"In case we simply do nothing and wait here until they arrive in our solar system, they will first go to the moon. There they will approach the destroyed cruiser to find out who or what caused the destruction. As soon as they have determined that the attackers originated on Earth, they will proceed to attack us here. But since robot ships of a galactic empire would be programmed to think in terms of entire planets, we cannot expect them to try to determine which of the inhabitants of this planet actually sent the H bombs to the moon. They will annihilate the whole planet.

"But what will happen if we interfere with the approaching robot ships? What will their reaction be if they determine that the enemy is still somewhere in the vicinity of the destroyed object? They will proceed to attack him, of course! We know that the robots are skillful tacticians. They won't pursue our small auxiliary vessel, all five of them at the same time. One of their number will be entirely sufficient for this purpose, namely, to seek us out and turn us into dust.

"This is where our only hope lies! We have no chance whatever to overcome the robot ships when all five are together. But if we succeed in separating them and then engage each singly, the odds will no longer be stacked against us."

Rhodan fully agreed with his friend Reg. Bell's reasoning even tore Khrest out of his lethargic state and seemed to instill a trace of hope in him.

Thora, on the other hand, remained silent as before. But she looked a trifle less self-possessed than she had a short time previously.

They continued discussing Bell's plans. Rhodan added more details. Thus they created a program that could be fed into one of their computers for evaluation and detection of possible errors, for which the machines would also supply the corrections.

This very evening Rhodan became involved in a strange conversation.

During the afternoon, Lieutenant Klein had reported that all the three big power blocs were preparing for a state of readiness in case of an atomic attack from outer space. They made preparations so that large populations could be evacuated from endangered areas within a few hours, if the necessity should arise. Rhodan was filled with satisfaction at hearing this news. From the time the robot ships were sighted there would elapse at least several hours until they would have determined what had happened on the moon and who the culprit was. Then, of course, they would fly toward Earth to destroy it.

This same evening Thora visited Rhodan. For the first time since they had been living aboard the same ship, she came into his cabin.

Rhodan was startled to such a degree that Thora could not fail to notice it. "It's amazing, isn't it, Rhodan?" she inquired with slight sarcasm.

"You're right, Thora. It is amazing!" Rhodan replied. "Why have you come here?"

"I have something to propose to you."

Rhodan motioned toward a chair. "Sit down, please. You have no idea how pleased I am to listen to you."

Thora seemed startled, but she could not detect any trace of sarcasm in his voice. She sat down in the chair and leaned back. "In another five or six days, Rhodan, your dream of a united world and of becoming heir to a galactic empire will come to a sad end."

Rhodan did not interrupt her, although he did not agree with what she said.

"In a few days," she went on, "our robot cruisers will

appear and discover what caused the destruction of our exploratory cruiser on the moon, and then they will turn the planet Earth into a highly radioactive rubble heap, destroying all the inhabitants at the same time. There are only a few people that are worth saving from this holocaust. And you, Rhodan, are one of those!"

Rhodan, who had been listening attentively, leaned forward as if he could run after her words, capture them in order to hold them once more close to his ear and listen to them again.

"Who? Me?"

Thora looked very serious as she resumed speaking. "Yes, you, Perry Rhodan! And perhaps also your friend Reginald Bell, since he has had the advantage of our hypnoschooling. Maybe Haggard, too, because of his medical knowledge that enables him to cure leukemia. And finally Tako Takuma, who has such remarkable faculties. I am herewith offering to save all of you. As the commanding officer of an Arkonide exploratory ship I am authorized to do so. You will be brought back to Arkon with us. We will find some use for you there."

Rhodan began to guess what was really at the bottom of all this talk. "What makes you assume that we are worthy to be saved?"

"Your special talents," replied Thora without hesitating. "They would mean a valuable addition for our Empire. You could be employed wherever vitality was desirable. You have this quality, as well as the special knowledge of our superior Arkonide technology. And the others, those like Tako Kakuta, could undergo the same hypnotraining that you and Bell have received."

Rhodan remained expressionless. "Did you also consider our usefulness for possible breeding purposes to create a new racial strain?"

She did not seem to notice his biting irony. "I can't imagine," she resumed, cooler than before, "that any female Arkonide citizen would even remotely consider any intimate relationship with a member of the human race."

Rhodan looked at her and uttered one comment: "Ahem!"

Then he waited. Thora had a tremendous capacity for

patience. It was almost fifteen minutes before she made as laconical a comment as he: "Well?"

Rhodan got up and walked over to the video screen that was set in the wall of the cabin instead of a window. He gazed at the limitless expanse of the desert sand in front of him. The stars in the sky were shining, illuminating the landscape with a dim light. This light created a diffuse shadow that made the furrows and depressions in the soil appear deeper than they were.

"Listen to me, Thora!" said Rhodan with determination. "One handful of this dry desert sand is worth more to me than all your decaying Empire. I am not at all interested in obtaining some more or less important position in your realm. I am solely concerned with this world here. And can you guess why?"

He turned around on his heels. "All we need to do is wait a little while longer. Maybe three or four thousand years. What does this time span mean in comparison with the long way we have come since the Stone Age? At the end of this time we will get the ruins of your whole Empire for a song! I would not want to be the person who taught the Arkonides the tricks that would enable them to delay temporarily the advance of the human race. Not stop it, only delay it."

He advanced toward her a couple of steps.

Cold rage was rising in her. She wanted to get up and leave so that she would not have to listen to his words. But his voice seemed to affect her suddenly as if she no longer had a will of her own. For the first time Rhodan was unconsciously endowing his utterances with the suggestive power that was a result of the hypnotraining he had undergone. His voice kept her chained to her seat.

"You see what will happen if we don't succeed in beating back your robot ships? They will attack Earth and annihilate us. But some of us will survive. Maybe a hundred, a thousand, or even a million. These people will never be able to forget what has been done to their fellow human beings. They will be possessed by the thought that nothing like their own fate will ever befall their descendants. You don't realize the extent of our vitality yet! It will take about 2,000 years for the human race to catch up again with our present level of development. But in the meantime your galactic Empire, which is already ripe with decay, will have to face us as an enemy. The odds will then be all in our favor; there is no doubt about the outcome of this confrontation. It will be a fight to the bitter end, because for as long as we can go back in our history, we have always kept battling against our opponents to the death. It will not be any different in the future war against your Galactic Empire, but then the human race will end up becoming the rulers of your realm."

Thora tried to gather up all her strength in order to leave the room. Before she had reached the door, however, Rhodan had started to speak again, and he kept her rooted to the spot.

"But we are not that far yet. You know as well as we do that there is a solid chance that we might wipe out the robot ships. They will believe us to be the harmless survivors of the cruiser explosion. They might even perhaps take us aboard their robot vessel in a rescue mission, before attacking our planet. That will provide us the right opportunity for action. There is still hope for us here; we are far from being lost!"

She tried to advance a couple of steps toward the cabin door, but he yelled, "Stay where you are!"

The brutal energy of this command gave her a violent headache. She whirled around.

But to her utter surprise he was just smiling at her. "Here on Earth we know of many cases like yours. Young girls that have been brought up in a sheltered, wealthy environment and who one day find out, to their utmost horror, that the majority of mankind lives in poverty and must struggle for sheer survival.

"You are not at all different from these young girls in your attitude. You feel compelled to despise us for the simple fact that we are a younger race than your own.

"The day that you come to me and tell me how foolishly you have behaved during the past weeks, I will confess how much I am in love with you, Thora!"

Now she was utterly confused. She wasted some precious moments trying to make up her mind whether to reply.

Finally her pride won out. She turned abruptly and left the room.

His declaration had shocked her far more than she cared to admit to herself. For on Arkon during the course of many thousands of years the rules of the game of love had been subordinated strictly to the laws of reason. It would have been considered a sign of mental disease if a man had confessed his love for a woman after having scolded and insulted her but a short while before.

She understood, however, despite her anger, that it was not possible to apply the same standards here on Earth. She sensed that Rhodan's timing of his declaration of love was part of a skillful maneuver. She felt quite helpless in the face of such calculated illogic.

For the first time she recognized with clarity how terribly young the human race really was and the amazing and horrifying forces that were hidden in that youth.

The big event they had been awaiting came two days later. Rhodan had not heard anything more from Mercant. That meant that no further developments had taken place among the big power blocs. Those in charge were waiting for the threat from space to materialize.

Manoli was sitting at the radio. The robots had finished their work and returned to their stations, where Khrest switched them off for the night.

Thora kept very much to herself. She made a point of avoiding Rhodan. Rhodan knew why.

Bell and Haggard played interminable games of chess.

Manoli was mostly bored. The Arkonide auxiliary vessel had excellent receiving sets. He could listen in to everything without difficulties whether it was the Peking police shortwave broadcasts or the news from the space station Freedom I or the longwave broadcasts of international senders. But the news had become rather dull in the last few weeks, and this post at the radio was no longer entertaining for Manoli.

But things changed radically that day! Manoli was just listening to a program of the space station, when it was suddenly interrupted by an important message from the announcer. "Squirrel to Aphid, Squirrel to Aphid. Located an unidentifiable object, direction phi 210, Theta 89. Distance 2 x 10^6 yards, speed about 2 x 10^4 yards per second. Shape cannot be determined. The object is approaching the moon. Over."

Aphid promptly confirmed receipt of the message and requested, "Send all further news in code!"

Manoli had taken down the message in shorthand. He tore the note off his writing pad and ran out of the cabin. He raced at high speed down the corridor toward Rhodan's cabin and could hardly wait until Rhodan let him in.

Manoli read the note to Rhodan, who reacted in a very excited fashion that puzzled Manoli.

"That's incredible!" Rhodan exclaimed.

Then Rhodan no longer paid any attention to Manoli; he called Khrest via intercom, asking him to come over to his cabin. Only then did Rhodan turn again to Manoli. He commanded, "Inform Tako to watch out for Klein's signals. We will soon find out more about this."

Manoli nodded briefly and left. Khrest appeared in Rhodan's room a moment later.

"We intercepted an announcement from the space station that an unidentified object is approaching the moon, coming from the direction of Mars," said Rhodan calmly. "I would like to hear your opinion, Khrest."

Khrest listened attentively to Rhodan's words and then inquired, "Any further details you can give me?"

"Speed 2 x 10^4 yards per second."

"Shape of object?"

"Unknown."

Khrest gazed at Rhodan.

"Thanks to the hypnotraining you should suspect the same as I do, Rhodan. Our base on Myra IV is no longer in the hands of the Galactic Empire. The approaching spaceship is not one of our robot cruisers but must originate from some rebelling part of our colonial fleet. Its crew appears to be rather inexperienced."

"Let's hope this spaceship is alone!" added Rhodan.

Within half an hour Klein had arrived with some additional information. In the meantime the strange object had come nearer and it was possible to recognize its shape.

While Klein conversed with Tako at the perimeter of the energy dome, more bits of news were received constantly, which Klein deciphered on the spot with the help of an automatic decoding mechanism that he carried on him. Tako had a receiver set that picked up the new data, which Manoli transmitted to him as soon as he obtained them himself via the powerful Arkonide communications apparatus.

The unknown object was spindle shaped, like two torpedoes that had been cut through the middle and then put together again with their pointed ends facing each other.

Rhodan listened in to what Klein was deciphering. He knew that spindle shaped ships belonged to the older models of the Empire and that their use was generally discontinued except in remote colonies. This proved to him what he had already suspected—the unknown approaching vessel could not possibly be one of the expected robot ships.

Khrest confirmed Rhodan's suspicions by adding, "The Fantan people own a number of spindle shaped transport vessels; they can't afford better ones. I am positive that this is a Fantan boat. The Fantan group is not too far from our Myra base. They might have occupied Myra IV and intercepted our emergency signal coming from our destroyed cruiser on the moon."

They found the final proof for their identification of the Fantan ship in the fact that it did not shield itself against radar or optical detection. The spindle shaped Fantan ship came closer to the moon, at miserably slow speed, as if it were alone in the universe and had nothing to fear from anywhere or anything.

This one Fantan ship was the only craft that had come into Earth's corner of the universe.

Thora had plugged into the telecom circle and had heard everything that Klein was reporting from the outside. When Tako returned from the meeting with Klein, Rhodan sent him to Thora's cabin to ask her to come for a discussion of the situation. The Japanese found Thora lying unconscious on the floor. The disappointment had proved too great a shock to her delicate system.

CHAPTER EIGHT

One hour later Lieutenant Klein announced more startling news. "The chiefs of defense request an interview with Mr. Rhodan!"

Rhodan was surprised to hear this. "Which chiefs?" he barked.

Klein seemed to find his reaction amusing. "A supranational security committee came into existence just a few minutes ago, sir. The chairmen are Ivan M. Kosselow from the Eastern Bloc Secret Service, Mao-tsen of the Asiatic Defense Forces and last but not least Allan D. Mercant, our patron saint."

Rhodan grasped the implication at once. "I'll be willing to receive these gentlemen without delay. When can they be here?"

"They are all agreed that things are most urgent. Mercant is already in Peking. He and Mao-tsen can travel here in about forty-five minutes. Kosselow won't take much longer to get here."

Rhodan thought for a moment. "Well, Lieutenant, announce the people as soon as they arrive. If need be I can let them in here one after the other."

Exactly one hour after this discussion the chiefs of the terrestrial secret services arrived at the Arkonide auxiliary vessel in the Gobi Desert.

Rhodan arranged for Khrest to participate in the meeting.

Rhodan learned that the evacuation of the population, as well as the most important industrial concerns, was already in full swing.

"We would like to find out from you, Rhodan, how much sense all these precautionary measures really make under the circumstances," said Mercant, "if you take into consideration the likelihood that the attacking robot ships will most probably make a hypercritical reactor out of this whole planet."

Rhodan enlightened Mercant about the conjectures he and Khrest had arrived at regarding the approaching ship. "I am presenting the facts to you the way they really are," he added. "We have a good chance to get rid of these attackers with one single well aimed shot.

"But if you should then give the all clear signal, you would make a grave mistake. For we must count on the possibility of failing with our counterattack measures, as hopeful as they might seem to us.

"In addition to that, I do not believe that we will have to face only a single enemy ship. Even if we should succeed in destroying it, others will surely follow, ones that will have intercepted the automatic emergency signal sent by the bombed Arkonide cruiser. In case we should overcome the first enemy onslaught we would gain a short breathing spell of a few weeks or at most a few months. We must utilize this brief span to get ready for the next attack, without having to cope with any additional risks."

Rhodan gazed intently at Mercant. "You know very well what I am referring to with this remark, Mercant! The nations of this world can no longer afford to keep up the embargo against the Third Power. We are the only people who are capable of protecting this planet against the threatening attack. We must have full freedom of action in order to make efficient use of the means that we have at our disposal to defend Earth."

Mercant looked at the two men who had come with him. Then he turned to Rhodan. "As far as the NATO group is concerned, we no longer consider the embargo to be in force from this moment on. We would also like to assure you that we place full confidence in you in all matters relating to the defense preparations for the impending enemy attack from space."

Rhodan's face bore an expression of utter amazement. The same moment Kosselow declared, "My own government shares the views just expressed by Mr. Mercant."

Mao-tsen added smilingly, "My people, too, join the other two governments in lifting the embargo against the Third Power, Mr. Rhodan."

Rhodan's reaction was one of complete surprise. He was overwhelmed by the unexpectedly swift acceptance of his suggestion. Then a slight smile played around his lips as he said with a hint of sarcasm, "Gentlemen! From the moment your governments are willing to extend the same confidence they show in us regarding the defense measures we will take against the threatening danger to all other areas —from that moment on, the Third Power will cease to exist. We will abandon this base here in the Gobi Desert and put at mankind's disposal all we possess and all the knowledge we have obtained from the superior Arkonide technology."

The discussion proceeded along the lines of working out the necessary details. Rhodan described his plans for intercepting the approaching hostile spindle ship while it was still in outer space. But in case these plans should fail, he gave instructions how to protect the inhabitants of Earth. Mercant, Kosselow and Mao-tsen were busy taking down notes.

As a conclusion to the meeting Rhodan declared, "Gentlemen! I wonder whether you realize that you cannot count any longer on the support of the Third Power in case we should not succeed in annihilating the spindle ship. This is a fight to the bitter end. Whoever loses will lose not only the battle but also his life. Since we must reckon with such an eventuality, I have written down some of the matters that are important for mankind to know. This document will be deposited in a safe place, where it will weather the impending attack on our planet.

"I am confident that these notes will be of help to mankind. In case of almost total destruction these descriptions should give a good start to the survivors of the holocaust. From this day on we must never forget that we are not the only living beings in the universe. We must accept the fact that other races exist, and we must be prepared to recognize that some of them will be hostile toward us.

"With this in mind I have described some of my recently acquired knowledge of matters."

The documents turned out to be quite lengthy, costing precious hours for Rhodan to complete. In the meantime the spindle ship had reached the moon's orbital path. It remained in the same orbit, following the moon at a constant distance of about 6,000 miles.

Rhodan had called his men in for a short meeting. Thora did not join them. She needed rest. Rhodan's suggestion that Tako and Dr. Manoli should remain behind on Earth was generally accepted. The two would find safe refuge there within the energy dome in the Gobi Desert. There they would be completely protected against any attacking force and possible later radioactive contamination. Tako received Rhodan's document for safekeeping with the promise to hand it over to mankind, or whatever remained of it, only at such a time as there was no longer any doubt that Rhodan and his companions had been destroyed, together with their ship, during the battle with the approaching invaders.

Tako and Manoli took up quarters in the former *Stardust 1.* Rhodan started out immediately afterward on his mission.

They ascended in the Arkonide auxiliary vessel to a height of about sixty miles. Rhodan had mapped out a plan of action that could not be accomplished with the automatic guidance system. Reginald Bell was his co-pilot, and Haggard and Khrest stayed in the central cabin.

The ship hovered motionless. The light of the automatic controls was dark. A small screen in front of them showed the position of their ship in relation to Earth's surface. All instruments except the altimeter registered zero.

Only the panel where Bell was sitting was illuminated, by five shining green bulbs. They indicated that the five nuclear storage condensers, each a giant of its kind, were charging and storing up their energy for the right moment when their full potential would be needed and discharged.

This stored up nuclear energy would be sufficient to surround the auxiliary vessel with a hypergravitational field that would insulate it from its surroundings. It would thus also take it out of the four dimensional space time continuum. A body inside such a hypergravitational field no longer existed within normal space. It passed into a space system of a higher order, which was subject to the same physical laws, although of quite different values. Rhodan had called this superspace system "the path behind the curvature of space" when he had learned about it during his hypnotraining sessions. This also explained the principles of the problems of hyperflight. Any body, such as the Arkonide ship in this instance, could penetrate into this superspace system by piercing through the convex surface of the space time continuum, then proceed in a straight line and, once at its destination, come out again through the surface.

But no one had ever tried to cover a distance of more than a light second by means of such a hyperjump. The difficulty in this case was that the relatively small auxiliary vessel was not equipped to store sufficiently large amounts of nuclear energy. Therefore, it would need enough time after the completion of its jump through hyperspace to store up new energy again. Its storage capacity was exactly calculated to provide energy for twice penetrating the space time surface. After the completion of one set of jumps, the craft needed a certain period of recuperation before resuming its flight. But unless their jump placed them in the exact spot Rhodan had calculated, this needed pause would afford the enemy enough time to locate them and assume a favorable position for attack.

According to Rhodan's calculations their jump should terminate within the shadow of the moon. The spindle shaped ship of the Fantan people still remained on the same course as before. It moved along the orbital path of the moon, still maintaining a distance of 6,000 miles behind Earth's satellite. The auxiliary vessel, however, would reappear in front of the moon.

Rhodan placed his hand on the red pushbutton that would initiate the jump. Then he pushed down hard on it. The button clicked softly; then the video screens grew suddenly dark, without any transition whatsoever.

This lasted just one second; then the video screen lit up again. The image on the screen had changed. In front of the ship appeared the thin crescent of the moon, illuminated by the sun, which had just come out from behind Earth.

Rhodan leaned back in his chair.

Khrest looked at him with a radiant expression on his fine face. "Excellent!" he exclaimed with admiration.

Rhodan did not rest. As soon as five minutes had passed—the time they needed for recharging the storage condensers with a minimal amount of energy—he started up the engines again.

The rest seemed like child's play. Rhodan steered the

space sphere into a crevice of the huge mountain wall of the crater in whose center lay the remains of the wrecked Arkonide cruiser. He was convinced that the Fantan people would eventually risk approaching the wreck and that he and his companions would be safest waiting for this moment while hidden in the deep shadows of the crater wall.

Khrest had asked to be excused from any participation during this enterprise. Rhodan had granted his wish, since he knew the mentality of the Arkonide scientist. The era in which they had built their galactic empire had long since gone. Fighting represented an action horrible beyond belief for the Arkonides, grown old.

Haggard was stationed at the radar, Bell at the artillery of the ship, while Rhodan remained at the steering console, in case he had to maneuver it manually.

The auxiliary vessel carried two types of artillery—weapons with a range of up to one light minute and those with a shorter range.

Rhodan was reluctant to use the farreaching rockets. Although the Fantan ship was of an old-fashioned type and equipped with rather weak defensive fields, one still could not discount the possibility that they might have installed some improvements before undertaking such a dangerous trip. These farreaching missiles were also liable to be detected too early. This would allow the Fantan people to evade them. Judging by what Rhodan knew of their mentality, the crew would not make a stand and fight but would probably turn and flee. But Rhodan was determined to force a decisive victory and not one that included the likelihood of the opponent's flight.

Some hours went by. Khrest was lying down resting, his eyes closed tight.

No word was spoken. Haggard sat in front of his radar screen, which remained blank, while Bell had his place before a panel covered with a series of buttons and wheels, his battle station.

Only once did Bell speak up. "I don't like this at all, Perry! We should take off and attack them. I'm not keen on lying here in ambush to wait for the enemy to make a wrong move."

"Nonsense, Reg!" answered Rhodan. "I don't want to run

any unnecessary risks, and besides, you know what the Fantan people are like, don't you?"

There were no more discussions after this. Many hours passed. Rhodan felt a strong desire to get up and see how Thora was getting on. But he was too much aware that the quiet hours they had been lying in wait could change within one second.

"Here they are!" said Haggard suddenly. "Location phi 15, theta 30."

"What speed?" Bell asked.

"Fifty yards per second in direction phi zero. Distance 500 miles."

Rhodan turned to Bell. "What is our position?"

"Favorable. That means we could lift up a few yards to get to the rim of the crater wall."

The boat started upward. It glided close to the wall of the pitch dark crevice in the crater mountain range, until it reached the rim of the towering rocky bulwark.

"Stop!" Bell called out. "That will do!"

This very instant the spindle shaped enemy ship became visible on the screen. Rhodan examined it thoughtfully. It was still about 500 miles away. It hardly seemed to move. The Fantan people were very cautious and preferred to creep up slowly on their target. This tactic must appear to them safest, the only chance to make sure of attaining a certain measure of security.

The Fantan ship was now sliding along at the same height as the rim of the circular range. They would have to ascend slightly to get over the edge of the crater wall. Such a maneuver would command a certain amount of their attention; therefore, it would be the right moment for the Arkonide vessel to attack the enemy.

Yet many hours would pass before they came to this point, considering the slow speed of the Fantan ship.

The circular mountain range was fairly small, with a diameter of about sixty miles in the center.

Rhodan kept hoping that they would concentrate their attention on the crater itself and not on the wall around it. There was no doubt that the dome of the Arkonide vessel showed itself for two yards above the protecting rim of the crater wall. That was not much, within the extensive rock formations, but still, it would be enough if the enemy was really alert.

Rhodan turned to Bell. "How do you plan to proceed?"

Bell pointed to a yellow switch and a hand wheel. "Neutralization of the crystal field," he replied. "All that will remain of their ship will be a whirling fog of hydrogen, carbon and metal atoms."

"How long will the bombardment last?" inquired Rhodan.

"I intend to let them have all we have."

"Is that really necessary?" asked Rhodan.

Bell was surprised. "Why, of course. I want to make absolutely sure."

"I would like to show something to Haggard," said Rhodan. "Just demolish their ship. The crew can't save itself, and they will no longer constitute a danger to us."

"Okay," agreed Bell. "I will bombard them for twenty seconds then."

Just then Haggard announced, "They appear to be increasing their speed; 100 yards per second, distance now about 350 miles."

And in the same breath he added, "What do you want to show me, Rhodan?"

"Something that should prove to be most interesting to you as a scientist. Just wait and see."

Tension mounted; yet time seemed to advance more slowly. The enemy ship grew bigger on the screen and showed its immense dimensions. Rhodan estimated its length to be about 1,000 feet. In the middle it was narrowed down to a diameter of approximately 100 feet. Even though this was an old-fashioned model, it was most likely far better equipped than the Arkonide auxiliary vessel. Unless Rhodan and his crew succeeded in destroying this formidable opponent, the fate of Earth appeared to be sealed. Rhodan was not confident about the future of mankind in case of defeat, despite what he had so firmly asserted in his talk with Thora.

"Two hundred fifty miles!" announced Haggard now, after what seemed an endless interval.

At 60,000 yards, Bell would start shooting.

Rhodan did not think that the Fantan people had located them. It was against their nature to continue their flight after having determined the presence of an enemy.

Nevertheless . . .

"One hundred and eighty thousand! They are increasing their speed!"

And a few minutes later Haggard called out, "They have stopped! They are not advancing any more!"

Rhodan reacted immediately. "Fire!" he commanded.

Bell hit the switch of the decrystallization field and then yelled, "Let's get out of here fast! We must go up higher!"

Rhodan started the ship instantly. With a sudden jerk he pulled the craft up beyond the rim of the crater wall and shot up to a height of several hundred feet. All the while Bell kept firing away.

His aim was perfect. The telescope screen showed the picture of the destruction of the Fantan ship. It was incapable of moving. The crystal structure of its outside wall crumbled away, and the nose of the craft dissolved to dust. Bell's weapon kept on devouring the Fantan ship and made inroads into its center.

Suddenly yellow lightning flashed from across the miles toward the Arkonide ship. Rhodan was blinded by the bright lights and closed his eyes for a second. When he looked again at the video screen he saw the landscape bouncing around madly.

They were still shooting! Incredible! They had hit the energy mantle around the Arkonide ship and caused it to vacillate wildly.

"Faster!" hissed Rhodan.

Bell did not react. With deliberate concentration he directed the decrystallization ray, which continued with its destruction of the hull of the Fantan craft.

There was another salvo coming from the enemy vessel. The shot glanced off the energy screen surrounding the Arkonide spaceship, causing it to vibrate violently under the impact. Bell's directional beam lost its aim for a while but then regained it and finished with its destructive work.

Nothing remained of the outside wall of the enemy vessel. At the same time all its generators were pulverized. Whatever remained—some parts of the equipment, interior walls, doors, instruments and the bodies of its crew—fell crazily whirling to the ground.

Bell breathed a sigh of relief. "Mission accomplished!" he shouted jubilantly.

Rhodan flew at low altitude across the center of the moon crater, past the wreck of the Arkonide cruiser, and approached the spot where the Fantan spindle ship had just been annihilated.

Haggard had left his post at the radar equipment and was peering intently at the video screen.

"What I want to show you, you won't be able to see from here, Haggard," remarked Rhodan. "Wait until we land."

He put the ship down close to the circular area on which the metal dust of the strange craft and its few remaining objects had settled.

While he was closing the helmet of his Arkonide protective suit, Rhodan said, "Come along with me, Haggard!"

Haggard was ready at once. They left their ship and flew with broad jumps to the spot where the biggest heap of wreckage lay.

There was not much to be seen of the crew. Apparently they had been surprised by the attack with opened space suits. Their bodies as well as their suits had been shredded to fine pieces through the explosive decompression when the outer hull of their ship dissolved.

Haggard found something that looked like a piece of skin. "Is that all that remains?" he asked with obvious disappointment.

Rhodan simply shrugged his shoulders. "I believe that should give you enough to go on in your examination."

Both men returned to their spaceship. Rhodan debated whether to visit the wrecked Arkónide cruiser once again and silence the automatic emergency signal or to fly back to Earth and bring the good news of the outcome of the battle to mankind, which had been unable to watch the fight, since it had taken place on the far side of the moon.

Rhodan decided on the second alternative. His reasoning was: The same instant that the Fantan ship had realized it was being attacked, its hypersender had broadcast an emergency signal out into space, just as the Arkonide cruiser had done before. There could be no doubt that the SOS call of the spindle shaped ship was beamed in such a way that it had to hit its receiver. Therefore, it was out of Rhodan's hands to prevent a further arrival of hostile forces from outer space.

A process had been set in motion that could no longer be influenced, let alone controlled or stopped, by anything Rhodan could undertake against it.

This was an additional reason for Rhodan to hasten his return to Earth. From now on the minutes would count even more than before. Their next opponent would certainly surpass the first Fantan ship in number and in cunning.

There was a flurry of excitement during their return flight to Earth when Haggard examined the skin shreds of the Fantan people with the supermicroscope of the Arkonide ship.

"Their skin is like leather," he explained excitedly, "and it is covered with fine scales. The fleshy remnants that are attached to this skin piece show a quite different structure and segmentation from the muscles of man or any other known animal species."

Rhodan smiled with amusement as he asked, "So what conclusions do you draw from all this, Haggard?"

"There must be a considerable biological difference between the human and Fantan races."

"Can you imagine what these creatures look like?"

"Unfortunately not. These few skin pieces don't give me enough of a clue."

"Well then, imagine a cylinder with rounded off ends, my dear Haggard," Rhodan began to lecture in professorial tones. "This cylinder is elastic to a certain degree and is completely covered with fine scales. In its upper part this cylindrical body contains several openings, which to us would look like so many dark holes. But in reality they do fulfill the functions of eyes, nose and mouth.

"Six identical extremities branch off this cylinder at various places. They serve as organs of locomotion, food intake and the usual functions of our own legs and arms. The only difference is that there is no difference between the Fantan people's extremities; they are all alike.

"The Fantan race is asexual and is propagated by a

process similar to one known in some of your houseplants, Doctor Haggard, where a branch of a shoot off the parent plant gives rise to a new offspring.

"This is what the Fantan people look like. Did you assume that all intelligent races from the universe must have the same appearance as you or me or Khrest? In time we will meet up with intelligent living beings that will seem more repulsive to us than our toads or tapeworms."

On Earth the news of Rhodan's victorious mission was received with indescribable jubilation. The atomic alarm was terminated without delay and the population returned to their cities.

The interruption had cost the world's economy a total of $80 billion. But what was this cost compared with the tremendous progress the nations made toward a united mankind!

Shortly after landing back on Earth, Rhodan received the special envoys of the three big power blocs. They had come to tender their thanks in exuberant phrases. Each had brought along some high and impressive medal to honor mankind's hero, who only yesterday had been considered enemy number one.

Rhodan let them carry on with their ceremonies and waited patiently until it was his turn to speak.

"Gentlemen, I regret that I am unable to share your great joy. You can't realize yet, the way I do, that this encounter was but the first in a series of hostile confrontations with alien intelligent races that inhabit the universe. We were very lucky that we could ward off this first attack. But luck alone will not be sufficient the next time around.

"I am very happy that world opinion approves of the steps we, the Third Power, have taken. Not only that; they even bestow medals and honors on us," he added with a faint trace of irony in his voice. "But please relay this message to your governments—we have won only the first round of a war that might consist of a thousand or more battles. I want to emphasize in the strongest terms to all concerned parties that you are witnessing here the beginnings of a development that will stretch over centuries or even millennia. The decisions we make here today will affect the fate of mankind *for all time to come!*

"Take this message back home to your governments! Tell them that there is no ally more loyal than the Third Power as long as the welfare of the *entire* human race is concerned.

"We demand from them in return recognition and full freedom; for the time being we are the only power capable of preparing effective defensive measures to fight off the next attack from space."

He paused briefly and allowed himself the luxury of a faint smile. "Spread this message to the four corners of the world, gentlemen! Make mankind understand that a new chapter in the history of the human race has just started. We are forced to think in terms of thousands of years, for we might perish otherwise!"

The next day the first partial delivery of metal plastic sheets arrived from Pittsburgh. The delivery took place via the same route any businessman would have used for a normal shipment of goods from the United States to the Gobi Desert.

Rhodan looked at this as a sign that the governments had reacted favorably and acted in a hurry upon his wishes. It reinforced his hope that mankind would see the light shortly and realize the enormous energies it possessed if only it were united.

He saw himself close to achieving his preliminary goal of a united mankind. He marveled at the relatively short span of time in which this development had taken place.

He realized, though, that this progress had not drawn its strength from within itself. The automatic hypersender and the Fantan ship it had lured to this part of the universe had played important roles in accomplishing this process of unification of the formerly divergent factions of mankind.

That evening Rhodan received an invitation to participate in a conference of the three big power blocks in Cairo. The invitation was extended to him by the same special envoys he had met the previous day.

Rhodan accepted the invitation with a great deal of satisfaction, since it was proof of the posthypnotic effect his interview had left in the minds of the special envoys. These men did not know that from that moment on they had become so convinced of his arguments that they were now representing his views, rather than those of their own governments.

The Third Power had been asked to participate in the Cairo meeting, not as an observer, but as a full fledged member.

Still later that night he had a conversation with Thora. For the first time since the spindle shaped Fantan ships had been located by the space station Freedom I, she left her cabin. She came into Rhodan's room just as unannounced and unexpected as a few days earlier.

Rhodan offered her a seat. She accepted with a friendly smile.

"I have had a lot of time to think about a great many things," she said. "I am sorry for having acted differently than I should have in many instances."

Rhodan was startled. He had never believed she would get that far in examining her inner self.

"I am gradually realizing," continued Thora, "where the way that you have chosen leads. I have *complete* confidence in *you*. You are a born leader of men, and mankind will follow you. But as far as mankind itself is concerned, I cannot yet judge. The little I know of them is not encouraging. Up till now they have been busy mostly with cutting each other's throats. I am not sure whether your expectations in your brother man are really justified.

"To come to the point—in the future you will no longer have to contend with me as an adversary. I will sit back and wait to see what comes of your plans. Your plans are good. Perhaps, given sufficient time, your fellowmen will turn out to be that race which will become heir to the Arkonide Galactic Empire. But until the Earthlings have reached that level in racial development, I will wait with my final decision."

Rhodan stood up, walked over to her and stretched out his hand. "This is a human gesture," he said. "Take my hand! I want to express my thanks to you!"

With some hesitation she grasped his hand, then responded firmly to his sincere handshake.

"I respect your viewpoint, Thora," he replied, "and I assume that Khrest will react in the same manner."

Knowing full well ahead of time that she would protest, he said, "Please, Thora, don't misjudge Khrest. He is just as much a member of the Arkonide race as you are. Whatever he did so far was as an expression of his gratitude for our having cured him of leukemia. Perhaps he also had better insight than you in the situation. But he will remain an Arkonide for as long as he lives. He will never act like a human being."

He winked at her with a mischievous grin to signify that the serious part of their discussion had come to an end. "But as far as you are concerned, my dear, there is still hope!"

He did not care that his final remark might offend her. She made a face and left the cabin. He knew that her days of proud aloofness were numbered. And while he thought about this, he felt again how much he loved her.

Outside, the robots were busily storing the newly arrived metal plastic sheets.

What we need most urgently now, said Rhodan to himself, *is to obtain some scaffolding as quickly as possible. We must start immediately with the construction of a battleworthy spaceship. This is more important for us than anything else.*

THE MUTANT CORPS

CHAPTER ONE

"Perry!" boomed the voice of Reginald Bell in the low ceilinged room. Then he pushed the STOP button and turned expectantly toward the door. Soon Perry Rhodan entered the cabin.

"Stop yelling like that, Reg!" he reprimanded his ebullient friend. Rhodan's face showed no trace of the excitement he really felt. Only his eyes gave away how eager he was to hear the news. "I hope you have something vitally important to tell me."

Reginald Bell turned again to the tape recorder and depressed the REWIND button for about three seconds. "I received a message from Geneva for you. It came just a few minutes ago."

Rhodan stepped closer. "Did you get results already? I thought it would take the big powers at least a day to come to an agreement about us. If they got through so fast, they probably broke off negotiations without any result. Come on, Reg, let me hear it! What is it?"

"Just listen to that taped message and enjoy every second of your triumph!"

Reg started the tape and then settled comfortably in his chair.

"This is the secretary's office of the Federated World Powers. We are calling Mr. Perry Rhodan to inform him of the results of our conference. This communiqué will be broadcast at the same time over all stations for general publication.

"The representatives of the NATO states, the Eastern Bloc and the Asiatic Federation have conferred today about the international legal status of the so-called Third Power.

"The events of the past few days, especially those which happened outside Earth's gravisphere, have given rise to serious concern in all parts of our world. The undoubtedly hostile approach of a spaceship of an unknown extraterrestrial race constitutes a case of clear and present danger for all mankind. On the basis of thorough discussions by the delegates of the NATO, the Eastern Bloc and the Asiatic Federation, we concede to the Third Power that only thanks to their successful intervention, a total destruction of the hostile intruder's spacecraft on the moon has been brought about. Therefore, the participants in this conference deem it advisable to recognize that a certain loyalty was demonstrated by the Third Power toward the common interests of all men. We have therefore decided to recognize officially the Third Power as a sovereign government whose domain will extend within the limits of its present location in the Gobi Desert.

"Mr. Perry Rhodan is herewith requested to confirm receipt of this communiqué and to make suggestions for the establishment of diplomatic relations."

Bell stopped the tape and waited for Rhodan's reaction to the good news.

"We have made it, Reg!" he said almost humbly. "It seems that the nations are slowly coming to understand that their enemy is to be found somewhere out there in the universe, and not here on Earth from the Third Power.

"But these gentlemen in their high posts can just forget about our establishing extensive diplomatic relations. They would like to exchange with us a couple of dozen ambassadors. But we are a special case in world diplomacy. They have become used to this by now to some extent. And they will have to do so even more in the future. Take down this answer, Reg, will you?"

"Why not speak directly to them, Perry?"

"I have my reasons for that."

Reg simply shrugged. "All right, then. Go ahead."

"Tell them that I am very pleased to have received such a positive report and that I appreciate the insight that was displayed during the Geneva negotiations. But I will have to wait to take up diplomatic relations, since we are suffering from an acute lack of space in our tiny domain, which does not justify the presence of diplomatic representatives. However, contacts of any other nature will be welcome at any time."

"Thanks for this message, Perry!" Bell countered in desperation. "I'll have to rack my brain to express it in diplomatic language."

"You will have to answer at once, my dear friend! There is no time to waste in long deliberations. The big power blocs have demonstrated with today's meeting that a new wind is blowing. We must keep up with this new speed."

"Right, boss. Is there anything else you want from me?"

"Yes. You can request the Peking delegation in Geneva to make some proposals about selling us the land on which our sovereign state is situated. I definitely don't intend to lease this parcel of land from them. The Third Power must own its own land."

"How large do you imagine our new state is?"

"The site of the space sphere is to be at the center of our domain, which should have a radius of at least thirty miles."

With these words Rhodan turned and left the room. As important as these dealings with the other governments of the world were for all concerned, there were still more vital matters he had to attend to immediately.

He stepped outside. Far in the background of their tiny base was the building housing the gigantic positronic computer that had been transferred to this spot from the Arkonide vessel. This was the supercomputer whose microphysical reactions could determine the future history of mankind; the brain that would guide Rhodan in the decisions he would have to make.

Rhodan sped over to the computer building within seconds with the help of his special Arkonide suit. He entered the hall and walked directly to the machine that had been a present of the two Arkonides.

Rhodan knew that he was facing a problem of a greater magnitude than any human being had ever faced before. The problem he would feed into the computer today would surpass in significance any previous questions. This time the survival of the whole human race depended on it.

Rhodan busied himself at the control panel. A low hum, hardly audible, came from the machine. The brain had been activated. The brain was not subject to any mental influence, and it worked 100 percent according to the laws of logic. It was totally immune to influence by the significance of any problem it was asked to solve. It did not know any of the value judgments that were applied, at least unconsciously, by a human being. The brain was concerned only with the meaning and content of the matter fed into it. It calculated the probable solutions for the outcome of a football game or a political election with the same matter of course approach as the outcome of a worldwide war. If later events did not coincide with the answer given, the deviation was due solely to an incorrect way of asking the question. Therefore, everything depended now on how Rhodan formulated his questions.

First he made use of the imposing machine during his preparations in formulating the questions he would ask. This took several hours.

The memory part of the machine functioned in three ways: It presented the results with the help of its interpretation cells as the final product in pictures, spoken words and printed signals. At the same time all these answers were conserved as permanent records. The typed answer tape was wound on a reel automatically and marked with appropriate cues to its content. Sound and image were put on a parallel tape, where they were recorded and synchronized by electronic impulses.

Rhodan's preliminary examination provided an incredible result.

There were more than 22 billion possibilities from which mankind had to choose some sensible path for the future. But in no way was it simply a question of one solution being right and all the others wrong. The scale ranging from advantage to disadvantage ran across the screen in a wide spectrum. After more than a hundred further selective processes, there remained on the positive side more than a thousand possibilities. Rhodan had to search for additional limiting questions to narrow the field to the vital last question.

Many hours went by. His physical exertion was minimal;

yet he perspired profusely under the immense mental strain of the experiments he was conducting.

Late that evening that he received the answer to the threat of a new invasion. The answer came almost as a byproduct. He repeated the experiment five times before he could finally accept the solution with all its implications. . . . the invasion is already taking place . . . !

Rhodan called Bell via radio.

"How's it going with Peking, Reg?"

"They are hard to deal with. They're wasting my time with lots of petty details."

"Let's discuss this purchase of land for our territory at a later time. Something much more urgent has come up in the meantime. Leave your station at once and go aboard the space sphere. Instruct Manoli and our three friends from the secret defense services to join you there right away. The ship must be ready to start within the next ten minutes. No one is to leave the ship, even if I should turn up late. Give the alarm for the whole base."

The crew managed to get the Arkonide ship ready within ten minutes. Yet Rhodan did not arrive on board until midnight. He joined his crew in the command center.

"Reg, you will be the pilot. Start immediately! I must have a talk with Tako."

Rhodan switched on the screen and called Tako Kakuta in the main command station of the base. Tako's face appeared on the video screen.

"Yes, Mr. Rhodan, what is it?"

"We are about to leave the base. Observe our start and when the right moment comes, lift the energy screen for a few seconds to let us pass through."

"Okay."

The Arkonide auxiliary vessel shot straight up toward the sky and disappeared from Tako's view like a quicksilvery will-o'-the-wisp.

Reginald Bell turned toward Rhodan, while his hands carried out the necessary flight maneuvers with automatic precision.

"Won't you finally tell us what all this is supposed to mean, Perry? Eric and the others are already doubting my sanity because I rushed them over here and then had them wait for hours."

"I have talked with the 'brain' since this afternoon and have asked it vital questions. This is what took so long. We will need a guide through this maze if we are ever to find our way amongst the labyrinth of problems the future has in store for us."

"And have you found what you were looking for?"

"Yes, I did, Reg."

For a few seconds Rhodan seemed to be lost in thought. Then he looked straight at Bell. "We must search Earth's gravisphere at once at least as far as the moon's orbit. One of the answers of the brain said that the invasion has already started."

Manoli was the first to overcome the shock they all felt at Rhodan's news. "Do you mean by the same extraterrestrials we beat back and whose ship we destroyed on the moon just a few days ago?"

"We all know perfectly well that that battle was nothing but a preliminary skirmish. Thora's explanations have turned out to be correct. The faster than light transmitter of the destroyed Arkonide spaceship on the moon has mobilized the enemies of both our civilizations and has lured alien intelligences into our corner of the galaxy. Such a race as the Fantan people, bent on annihilation, will not be satisfied with half measures and individual actions. I have fed the information regarding our situation into the brain. The answer of the machine was that the invasion has already started. Will you please go now to your stations. You know what needs to be done!"

Whatever had not yet become routine in the running of the ship became so on this flight. The automatic scanner reported in regular intervals, "No foreign bodies can be located."

Rhodan regularly checked the stations manned by Bell, Eric Manoli, Captain Klein, Li Tschai-tung and Peter Kosnow.

At a distance of about 240,000 miles from the center of the Earth, Rhodan ordered the ship to enter an orbital path. He did not, however, let the sphere float without any power drive like a satellite. This would have resulted in an orbital period of almost five weeks. Instead, he had the sphere's drive thrusting at an angle to the orbital path, which canceled out the centrifugal force caused by the tremendous speed.

"That's fine!" murmured Rhodan as the gigantic crescent of the moon fell behind them.

"The computer is said to be infallible, isn't it?" asked Manoli suddenly as Rhodan stopped near his station. "Where, then, is our enemy if the invasion has already begun? As far as I know there is no field that can absorb the spy-rays of our spaceship."

"Only man is fallible," confessed Perry Rhodan. "If the invasion is not really taking place, I must have asked the question the wrong way. In this case I almost hope I have made a mistake."

"You have made one indeed," came Thora's voice over the loudspeaker. "You might just as well come back to Earth, Perry Rhodan. I have followed your endeavors here in my cabin, and I have observed what the scanners reported. There is no alien spaceship out here! You would be better advised to devote your energies to more urgent tasks on Earth!"

"Thank you for this advice. Is Khrest with you?"

"He is resting in his cabin. Both of us had decided not to participate actively in this mission."

The same moment Khrest spoke up via the intercom system. "I have listened in, Rhodan. Although I share Thora's opinion that there is no enemy craft out here in this part of the Earth's gravisphere, I do not agree that your question to the brain must of necessity have been wrong. The brain stated that the invasion has already started; it did not inform you, though, at what time the expected landing of the invaders would take place. It is quite possible that the enemy forces are still at a distance of many light-years from here. They might reach Earth only within the next few days. I have no objections to this patrol flight and I consider it a very good precautionary measure on your part. You should repeat it in regular intervals, if I might make this suggestion, Rhodan."

"You certainly may, Khrest! Many thanks."

"Shall I proceed with the landing?" inquired Bell.

"Circle once around Earth over both poles. And in the meantime you can tell me what you have been able to accomplish in your talks with Peking."

"Well, the Asiatic Federation believes that that desolate stretch of desert around the Goshun salt lake, exactly 102 degrees eastern longitude and 38 degrees northern latitude, is the most valuable piece of real estate anyone has ever imagined in his wildest dreams!"

"Have they quoted you a price already?"

"Why do you think I am so upset about these gentlemen? They are asking seven billion dollars! They do agree, though, on our request for a diameter of sixty miles across our territory."

"Did you tell them that we don't have that kind of money? One billion would have been more than enough!"

"These bloodsuckers are sitting on their high horse, and they won't give in a penny. It would be sheer waste of time to try to get them to come down in their price. They outright refuse to do so. We will just have to see how we can get that sum, Perry."

"Seven billion . . ." said Rhodan. "We need half of that sum alone for our assembly plants inside the energy dome. But we don't have that much money even for our important industrial needs."

Bell chuckled. "The mightiest government on Earth is also the smallest and the poorest. Quite a paradox, isn't it?"

"You are digressing, Reg. Kakuta has found a few productive suppliers of industrial goods for us. But they can't supply us with the money we need. We have only several ridiculously small bank accounts in some countries around the globe. What we need is a financial wizard."

"And even he would first want to find out about his salary from us. Whichever way we turn, Perry, we can't escape the fact that you must have the money before you can buy land, factories and materials and hire people. We must establish credit first of all."

"Don't we have any credit?" interjected Manoli. "Don't you know the old saying of our bankers—whoever has power has credit, too?"

"That bit of 'wisdom' implies the misuse of power," explained Rhodan. "It reminds me of armed robbery."

"There are spiritual weapons. None of us would approve if we were to threaten them with our superior means of physical destruction," commented Bell.

"But to acquire superior mental ammunition brings us back to what I said before—we need a sharp mind, a financial genius."

"We certainly show here no lack of superior minds," remarked Bell.

"Would you like the job of Secretary of the Treasury of the Third Power? Could you guarantee that you will influence the financial world market within half a year so that the Third Power will completely dominate it?"

"I am an astronaut, astronavigator, and electronic engineer. I have studied astromedicine and geology. I have undergone the same hypnotraining of the Arkonides as you did. I consider myself to be way above the average intellect. But as for money—I have never been particularly lucky at it."

"So you decline my offer of that high financial post in our government?"

"I definitely do. I have no ambitions along that line, Perry."

"There will be plenty of opportunity to prove your superior mind in other ways," Rhodan reassured him. "Just wait until we have landed. Then all of us here will meet together with Tako Kakuta. I have something special in mind for him to do."

The space sphere shot down almost vertically toward the Gobi Desert. The protective energy screen was opened for a brief time to let them pass through. As the mighty vessel touched down a faint pinkish glow appeared on the eastern horizon.

Eight men were assembled around the big table—Rhodan, Bell, Manoli, Haggard, Kakuta, Klein, Li Tschai-tung and Peter Kosnow.

All listened attentively as Rhodan addressed them. "Friends! I hardly need lose any time discussing our present situation. We are in possession of power and diplomatic recognition. On the other hand, we are quite destitute despite the beginnings of an industry of our own. In addition to that we are threatened any hour now with the onset of an enemy invasion from outer space. I have called you together here to tell you that you will be called upon to accomplish the utmost in the near future. I will have to demand from you a total commitment. Our job requires not only an enormous potential capacity of energy, but also speed and perfect reaction.

"You, Reg, will go to Peking with Tako Kakuta and conclude the negotiations for the purchase of our territory. You have already discussed how we shall pay the purchase price, namely, in monthly installments of 500 million dollars, so that we will complete payments in fourteen months.

"For the rest of you I would like to outline roughly a plan to speed up our industrial production and increase our output.

"But before we discuss any further details of this plan, would you please read this newspaper article. Then let me know whether you recall any additional data of the incident described here. Finally, present me with your ideas how we may make use of this affair for our own purposes."

CHAPTER TWO

The London night air was filled with heavy fog. A bone chilling humidity rose from the waters of the Thames, crept into the clothes of men and made them shiver.

Late that night, a shabbily dressed man crossed the Vauxhall Bridge, then walked along the left riverbank along Grosvenor Road. He had turned up his collar and pulled his hat down over his ears, as if he intended to hide his face.

Behind the gas works the man turned to the right, crossed St. George Square toward Lupus Street and then turned into Alderney Street.

He stopped before a heavy teak door and rang the bell.

An elderly heavyset lady opened it after a while and inquired what he wanted.

"I want to see Mr. Barry, please."

"I am sorry, sir. I can't possibly disturb him at this late hour. Mr. Barry is just ready to retire, and you see that I myself—"

"That you, too, were ready to go to bed. I am sorry to have disturbed you, but it's a different story with Mr. Barry. He won't think any more about going to sleep as soon as he sees me."

"Who should I announce, sir?"

"Don't bother announcing me. I know my way. Thanks a lot."

"How dare you!" exclaimed the outraged woman, as the man pushed ruthlessly through the scarcely opened door. Now the bright hall light showed up his rather questionable appearance. "Who are you? I can't let you come in!"

"Thank you very much, madam, and please don't bother yourself any more."

Hiram Barry was still sitting at his writing desk, not at all about to retire for the night. The light of his desk lamp illuminated the writing pad, and the rest of the room was in darkness.

"Didn't you want to go to bed, Milly?" said Barry as he heard the door open behind him.

"Milly *is* going to bed," declared the visitor.

The sound of his deep voice made Barry turn around, startled. Only a shadow was visible in the darkness, but the voice had given the intruder away. This voice was unforgettable for Hiram Barry.

"Adams," he moaned.

"Homer G. Adams," completed the visitor. "I hope that I did not come at an inopportune time."

"No, of course not, Adams. My house is open any time of the day for you. You know that certainly."

"The things that I do know are far back in the past. But I *do* remember them, and that is the important thing. Don't you agree, Barry?"

"You always had a very bright mind, Adams. You could have made a lot of money with your memory alone. I have always admired you and, of course, also envied you a little bit."

"And don't forget the hatred, Barry. I will accept admiration, and I don't mind even those that envy me, for vanity feeds on the envy of others. But hatred is a dangerous thing, as you can see in my example. I do not like people to hate me."

"What do you want, Adams? Don't talk about hatred that goes back so far. I don't hate you now."

"Of course you don't hate me any more. One can forget such things in fourteen years. I don't need to kill you any more, for your hatred has turned to fear, and with *that* I will gladly let you go on living. Perhaps this will pay back some of the debt you owe me. It's a terrible thing to have to live with fear."

"Did you come here to tell me that? Have you been thinking of hatred during all these fourteen years? I can't imagine that, for you would have perished thinking of nothing but hatred, and besides, wasn't it twenty years, if I'm not mistaken?"

"I was sentenced to twenty years, but after fourteen years they felt I had served enough time. I was let off because of good conduct. You should know *that*."

"Yes." Barry nodded. He had regained his composure somehow in the meantime. "May I offer you a drink?"

"If I could be quite sure that there isn't any poison in it."

"I wouldn't be that stupid, Adams. Please have a drink. I still recall how fond you used to be of whiskey. And now, tell me everything. I would like to know how matters stand between the two of us fourteen years later."

"Our relationship is no longer important. There is nothing to discusss about this, and neither is there anything interesting to report from my years in prison. I won't keep you long now, if we come to a quick agreement."

"What should we agree upon?"

"I need a suit. A good, new, fashionable suit."

"Is that all you want? Here's fifty pounds for that."

"The money will be in addition to all that, Barry. First the suit and then some pocket money. You might remember an account at the Midland Bank, way back. It amounted to 16,000 pounds. Not a big sum, I know. It was always my fate never to possess money of my own, apart from this small old age pension—the 16,000 pounds. I'm sure some additional interest has accumulated in the meantime."

"I don't know what you are referring to, Adams. How should I know anything about your accounts with the Midland Bank?"

"I'm referring to that account which we kept in your name. You might remember that the transaction with Servey, Ltd., showed some profit that could not be shown in your books."

"You mystify me, Adams."

"I can't see why you shouldn't understand that. Have you ever wondered why you escaped a prison sentence at that time? Have you ever asked yourself why Homer G. Adams refused to make a statement that, although it would not have exonerated him, would nevertheless have helped to have Hiram Barry sentenced for a long stretch of time? Do you seriously believe that I wanted to protect you so that you could spend my money? No, sir. The reason I let you escape was so that you could *protect* my money, and today I have returned to get my money back—including interest. If you deduct the cost for the suit, the amount should be about 24,000 pounds. In case you have speculated with my money, it might have even increased to two million pounds, but that doesn't interest me at all. All I need is the 24,000 pounds, and you can keep whatever you have earned with my capital in the meantime. I don't think that I am praising myself, Barry, if I say that I have treated you quite generously. You should rather have expected a much harsher reaction."

Barry hesitated with his answer. His fingers were grasping the edge of the table. "You know very well, Adams, that 24,000 pounds is a great deal of money, especially for someone like me. I have never lived in as grand a style as you did."

"It is, of course, anyone's privilege to live in the style he wants. You are a small crook, and no one has ever hindered you from becoming a big one. Besides, you seem to confuse two different things. If I ever swindled somebody out of twelve million pounds, I did it only with money that belonged to somebody else. My big deal that went into the billions had no personal avarice as a motive. I did it, let us say, because I like that kind of a game. I place great importance, Barry, on being considered an amateur and an idealist. I want to be recognized in the eyes of the world as a selfless servant for great things."

"Still to this day?" asked Barry.

Homer G. Adams nodded slowly. "Still today. Don't you believe for a moment that I will retire from the scene while I am still in the best years of my life. I shall return. I had a great deal of time to think, Barry, and I have heard quite a few things. But that would not really interest you too much. Give me the suit and the money, and then I will no longer bother you."

Hiram Barry seemed to have come to a decision. "Come up to my bedroom with me, Adams. You'll have half an hour to inspect my closets and look at my clothes."

Adams did not need half an hour to do that. It took him exactly three minutes to make up his mind.

"I'll take this one," he said. "You are hardly any taller than I am, and therefore, the jacket should fit me all right. I'll have to turn up the trouser cuffs a couple of inches, but nobody would notice that in the darkness, and tomorrow I will take the suit to a tailor. Where can I change clothes?"

"Over there is the bathroom."

"Thanks a lot, Barry. I see we understand each other. In the meantime, will you be good enough to write a check for me?"

Ten minutes later Adams returned to the library. A check had been made out for the sum of 24,000 pounds, and it bore Barry's flourishing signature, which could hardly be falsified.

"Would you need any cash, Adams?" Barry inquired politely. "You'll probably want to go to some hotel."

"Thanks a lot. You are very charming, my friend, but any prisoner is given a certain sum of cash upon his release from prison. In this respect our government shows itself to be rather generous. Therefore, you don't need to give me any more than is due to me. Homer G. Adams has remained the old skinflint that he was many years ago, but he still has his pride and will not accept alms from anyone. Well, so long, Barry. It was such a pleasure to see you again after all these long years and to have such an interesting chat with you."

After Adams had left, Hiram Barry dialed the telephone

number of the Midland Bank. He instructed the night clerk to deliver a certain message to the bank manager the very first thing the next morning. Then he dialed another number and announced himself, strangely enough, with a girl's name.

"What is that supposed to be, that you disturb me so late at night, lad? I was swamped with business deals all day long, and I had much too much to drink. Please call back again tomorrow, but not before dinnertime."

"Just a minute. You will sober up as soon as you have listened to me for a moment."

"Oh, stop that nonsense. I don't fall for such things."

"For heaven's sake, will you listen to me! You are in serious trouble if you put down that receiver now. I'll be over at your house in half an hour and break down your door and get you out of bed."

"What has happened?"

"I just had to write a check for 24,000 pounds, drawn against my account at the Midland Bank."

"Wait a minute! Have you lost your mind? Or did somebody break in and hold a gun on you? But whatever it is, my dear boy, call the bank at once and have them stop that check, and then you call up the police right away."

"I've already informed the bank, but I left quite a different message than you might think. I instructed them to transfer money from my other accounts, because this account has only 14,000 pounds in it right now."

The man at the other end of the line had sobered up completely by now. "Will you finally tell me what is going on? Did the devil in person come and get that check from you?"

"You are almost right. It was Homer G. Adams who was released from prison today."

The man at the other end of the line was struck dumb. Only after a few seconds did he manage to groan, "Adams has been released? Then for heaven's sake, don't talk with the police."

"Of course I won't talk with the police—only with you. That is your end of the business, and in case you don't remember the hours exactly, the bank will be open tomorrow morning at nine o'clock."

The first client to show up at the Midland Bank was Homer G. Adams.

He did not seem to notice the nervously jerking face of the bank teller. Adams stared at the ceiling of the large room with a very bored expression and seemed to be counting the many lightbulbs that adorned the beautiful chandelier. Adams was a man of great patience. That his eyes were nevertheless closely examining everything that went on around him could not be noticed by even a very critical observer.

Yet the little man with the big head was inwardly quite worried whether there was enough money in that bank account—Barry could have closed it out a long time ago. After all, it was in Barry's name.

After a few minutes, the teller returned.

"I'm sorry, sir. There seem to be insufficient funds in this account. We cannot pay you the full amount of this check."

"How much is the shortage?"

"About a hundred pounds, sir."

"Is that all? For that little sum you make such a fuss?"

"We have to keep our accounts balanced, sir," stammered the man behind the window.

"If you want to keep your accounts balanced, you could have given the owner of this account credit for a hundred pounds, couldn't you?"

"Yes, sir, we do that in general, but in this particular case we were instructed to close out this account after paying out the total amount that was in it."

"That's all right then. I'll be satisfied with whatever sum you have in that account, provided you don't make me wait more than five minutes."

After Adams got the money he left the area as fast as he could. He took the Underground to Picadilly Circus, where he got out and went shopping on Regent Street for all the things he needed. He had dinner at the airport in Croydon. To the waiter who was serving at his table, he appeared to be a very nervous and distrustful person. "Tell me, waiter, how long will it take? I must catch that jet to Tokyo."

"Your plane leaves at 1345, sir. You still have more than an hour and a half till then. You will have no difficulty whatsoever finishing your meal. We serve very promptly here."

Homer G. Adams did not seem quite convinced of that. He turned to a gentleman at the next table and called out with a loud voice, "Pardon me, sir. Are you taking the jet to Tokyo too? I mean the jet that leaves at 1345."

The man examined him and replied, "Sorry, I'm leaving at 1320, but not for east Asia."

"Excuse me," mumbled Adams.

Homer G. Adams ate his meal as quickly as he could. He kept looking at the big clock on the wall of the restaurant while swallowing every bite almost without chewing it. He asked for his bill as soon as the waiter served his dessert. He left the table while he was still chewing the last bite, paid the cashier and then walked over to the luggage counter.

"Pardon me, sir, but could you please check if my luggage is already aboard the plane?" He showed the clerk his luggage check.

"The jet to Tokyo," said the clerk. "The luggage is being put aboard this very moment."

"But are you quite positive that my suitcases are there too?"

The clerk took a deep breath and obviously had difficulty keeping his temper. "Of course your luggage is being put aboard, sir. You have the receipt. We are very reliable people, and it is not at all necessary to double check."

"I beg your pardon. If you say so."

Adams pretended to be satisfied, but in reality he was still deeply worried about another matter. He went to the gate and learned that the passengers were not yet permitted to pass to the airplane. Then he hurried to the exit at the north side of the airport and called a taxi.

"Take me to Epsom, please. Go as fast as you possibly can."

The driver raced at breakneck speed and received a generous tip at the end of the trip.

Homer G. Adams then hailed another taxi and asked to be taken to Dorking. There he hailed a third taxi and directed the driver to return to Croydon Airport. As he got into the cab it was 1335.

"Can you make it to the airport in ten minutes?"

"Impossible, sir."

"Try to do your best," encouraged Adams in a kind but urgent voice.

"But it is really not possible, sir. I know this area inside out. We will need at least thirteen minutes to get there if everything goes right."

"Okay, but drive as fast as you can. A jet is leaving for Tokyo at 1345. If we manage to see that plane leave, you'll get an extra tip of ten pounds."

"Do you want to catch that plane?"

"No. All I want is to see it leave the airport."

The driver did his utmost, and he was lucky not to run into much traffic. The taxi arrived at the north exit of the airport at exactly 1347.

Adams raced into the hall and observed the Tokyo jet disappearing in the midday sky. His face showed an expression of great satisfaction, quite in contrast with the gentleman next to him, who expressed his anger loudly. It was obvious that he had just missed the plane. Adams felt moved to address the man.

"Don't be so upset about this, sir. I, too, have missed the jet, but I know a way out of this misfortune."

"Who are you?"

"A fellow sufferer. I'm expected in Tokyo tonight, and I hope I can still meet my friends there at the time we arranged."

"Do you have a private jet?" asked the stranger, showing more interest.

"No. I don't have a private jet, but I know that another flight is leaving for Sydney, Australia, in twenty-five minutes. The plane will stop over in Zanzibar, and there we can catch another plane to Tokyo, coming from Cape Town, South Africa."

"Well, beggars can't be choosers. Many thanks, sir. This way we will still get to Tokyo before noon."

In Zanzibar they had a stopover of almost an hour. They went to the airport restaurant. Adams had found out that his companion's name was John Marshall and that he was twenty-six years old. Marshall had said nothing about his profession, and Adams was not interested in finding out, since at this moment he could not guess the significance of his meeting with this young man.

But the mutual game of hide and seek came shortly to an end. Adams bought a newspaper from a little boy. The paper came fresh from the presses and contained the very latest news.

On the second page Adams found a headline that did not surprise him much. After all, this occurrence had played a big role in his calculations, and he had been quite convinced that it had a high degree of probability. This news was extremely important for him and for John Marshall, too.

"Would you like to know what happened to the Tokyo jet we missed in London?"

"Well, what happened to it?"

"The jet exploded near Kiev and fell into the Black Sea."

"Are you serious?"

"Well, you can read it here, black on white." Adams handed the newspaper to his companion, who quickly glanced at the report.

"Well, we can consider ourselves lucky that we missed that plane," said Marshall.

"Yes, certainly. Life is much more important than the few material things we own. Nevertheless, I hope you were not carrying anything of value in your luggage."

John Marshall smiled enigmatically. "Nothing of importance, Mr. Adams. All that matters to me can be carried in this small bag, which I never let go. The clothing that I have lost in my suitcases can be easily replaced. I an not too worried that my luggage seems to have been destroyed, but I sincerely hope for your own sake that things are the same way with you, sir."

Adams felt Marshall's searching gaze resting on him, and he did not know what to make of it. Marshall was tall, young and healthy. His face bore a frank expression and bespoke undeniable honesty, but his eyes appeared far more mature than his chronological age would have led one to believe.

Since Homer G. Adam's trip was for top secret purposes, he took refuge in obvious silence. He did not answer Marshall's question but brought the conversation back to insignificant small talk, since he did not want to appear too rude.

Above the Indian Ocean the situation changed completely.

"You have a great deal of money with you, don't you, Mr. Adams?" said Marshall suddenly after a long period of silence.

"What makes you think so?"

"Because you are looking at your bag at regular intervals with the same attentiveness that I do. People don't usually turn their head to look up at the luggage rack that often if they have just a few sandwiches and a newspaper in their suitcase."

"That is most interesting. You seem to be interested in psychological studies, Marshall."

"That's right. I've been interested in psychology for a long time, but you are avoiding my question."

"If you are interested only in theoretical psychological problems, it could hardly be much of your concern whether I *really* carry a large sum of money with me."

"I only asked in your own interest, Mr. Adams. Provided you have a lot of money here with you, you should carry your suspicions much farther than you have so far. Then just looking at our bag won't be enough."

"As long as my luggage is up there on the rack, that is enough for me to know. That tells me that my money is still there. Or would you, being a psychologist, suggest a different logical conclusion to my thoughts?"

"Your little suitcase is new. It still carries the label from a store on Regent Street. I would bet you anything that you bought it only this morning."

"Absolutely right," said Adams, perplexed. "But what is that supposed to mean?"

John Marshall leaned over to him and whispered softly, "It is possible that someone else has purchased the same type of bag. If that bag, then, were in the luggage rack above us, your logical conclusion would not amount to much."

Adams just shrugged. He thought of the gun in his pocket, which he could use if Marshall tried to pull some dirty trick—which would hardly be feasible here, where there were eighty eye-witnesses present. "Okay," he said finally. "Obviously you would like to see a lot of money in one little suitcase. All right, I'll do you that favor."

He stood up, took a bag down from the luggage rack, sat down again and opened the little suitcase. That same instant, he had the same sensation he had had many years ago when he saw his big deal slip through his fingers.

He closed his eyes and counted to ten silently. That was an old habit that helped him to remain calm in critical situations. When he looked up again, he was once again the old, sober genius of the stock market who never lost his nerve.

"How come you knew my money had been stolen, Marshall? I demand that you speak up now without any further ado and that you leave out your rather doubtful psychological tricks."

"I believe it hardly matters any more how I knew this. You should rather ask who has the money now."

"And do you know where it is?"

"I have a pretty good idea, but I'd rather discuss this in quiet and peace with you. Would you like to accompany me to the lounge section? We can look then for a nice spot in a corner where we will not be disturbed."

They left. While they were on their way to the lounge, Adams stated, "I'd like to inform the chief pilot of the theft."

He returned in a short while. "Everything is in order—as far, at least, as my report of the theft is concerned. I hope that you can tell me more about it. The inquiries from the police can start only after we have landed. Perhaps they will close off the airport and not permit the passengers to leave, but that is not enough for me. I would prefer if we could take care of this matter ourselves, rather than wait for the police. We should try to find the thieves while we are still in flight. Who would you think is the guilty party?"

"I don't know, but I would suspect at least six to eight of our passengers here."

"You think they are here on board, or do you think that my bag was exchanged earlier, perhaps in Zanzibar? No—I looked into the case in the airport restaurant. Then everything was still in order. Therefore, the thief must be here on the plane. The only time the bag could have been exchanged was while we were boarding the plane. We were standing in line and advanced very slowly through the gate. It is possible that I put my bag down on the ground from time to time."

"I am inclined to agree. I share your thoughts there, but I really cannot tell who the guilty party is. We would have to suspect somebody who was close by while we were boarding the plane. I have closely examined these people several times already, but none of them has the same bag as you do."

"Very strange, indeed. Now you know so little, and yet just a little while ago you were so amazingly correct in your suspicions."

"Another question," Marshall said. "The amount you are missing might be quite large for the average person. Would this money be irreplaceable for you?"

"I don't quite get what you mean," replied Adams hesitatingly. Again he felt distrust for John Marshall. "Your formulations are often quite amazing, Mr. Marshall. On the other hand, I cannot imagine that the man who stole my money would behave as conspicuously as you do."

Suddenly the door from the passenger compartment flew open and several men came in noisily. Two of the men slammed the door and then bolted it, as if several other passengers wanted to get in too.

Almost all guests in the lounge section jumped up, completing the sudden confusion. There was so much noise and shouting that no one could hear until one of the men shouted loudly for everyone to be quiet. He emphasized his demand with a pistol.

"Everyone sit down!" commanded the stranger. "I have a few questions to ask you, gentlemen. Who of you carries a weapon? Please let me know immediately."

The first person to raise his hand was John Marshall. Several others followed suit, including, finally, Homer G. Adams. Altogether, seven people carried arms.

Someone asked what the meaning of all this was.

"Silence!" thundered the voice again. "We are in a very critical situation now. Several passengers have overwhelmed the ship's crew and have taken over. Some of these men have entered the passenger section to disarm all travelers. Our greatest concern now is to guard this door so that nobody can enter the lounge section. We want to hear suggestions how we can restore law and order on this plane."

"You can't lock that door," protested one lady. "My husband and my children are back there in the passenger section."

Several other passengers made similar protests, but they were in the minority, and their demands were ignored.

"We can't make any concessions now to individual wishes from you, gentlemen. We must ask you to exert self-control and to think of the danger we are in at this moment."

"It would be good," came a voice from the background, "if we did not overestimate the danger. Whoever resists these bandits might get the short end of the stick, but I don't think these criminals really want to threaten our lives. All they are interested in is our possessions. Therefore, I suggest we capitulate at once, for this is the only way to save our lives for sure."

"Coward!" someone called indignantly.

Another expressed suspicion. "You're probably one of these gangsters."

"It would be advisable if only one person spoke at a time," demanded John Marshall. "I believe that I can give you some enlightenment on what has happened here, but only if you make sure that the entrance to the passenger room is closely guarded."

Several armed men pushed toward the door and reassured him that they would be in charge of keeping that door firmly closed.

"Go on! Let us hear your explanation," urged the first speaker.

John Marshall said, "I'd like to say at the beginning that I do not know all this with absolute certainty, but I know enough for sure to suspect that this danger should by no means be minimized. The gangsters are undoubtedly out after our valuables, and in particular, they want to get at a sum of more than 23,000 pounds. They have already stolen this money."

"Why then all this hullabaloo? Do you think they will leave the rest of us in peace?"

"Most likely. They are probably hardly interested in your money—perhaps just in your wives' jewelry. But the greatest danger for us lies in the fact that the gangsters might make an attempt on the life of the man whose money they have stolen, for these criminals seem to believe that their only guarantee to really keep that money is to kill that man."

"And who is that person?"

"That doesn't matter here."

But Adams got out of his seat and bowed slightly to the group of excited passengers. "I am this man. Please forgive me if I have caused you such inconvenience by my mere presence on this plane, but in the final analysis I am an innocent victim of circumstances."

Adams felt Marshall's hand on his shoulder and sat down quietly in his seat. It would be better now if John Marshall carried on the discussion.

"Very soon we will be forced to proceed to action, ladies and gentlemen," Marshall said. "Therefore, will you please avoid any unnecessary questions now. The danger is the same for all of us here, as uninteresting as most of you are to these bandits. They have their eye on Mr. Adams, and in order to render him harmless, they will undoubtedly fly this plane to some other destination. That might be some deserted coast along the ocean, the middle of the Indian jungle, or even, perhaps, the highlands of Tibet. But taking all this into consideration, you will understand now that we *must* undertake something for our defense. As long as we are still airborne, there is no immediate danger, but this can change very rapidly."

So far none of the gangsters had tried to break down the door between the passenger section and the lounge section.

In the "unoccupied" section of the plane there was still another small group of the crew—two cooks, a waiter and three stewardesses.

Marshall walked over to them. "You probably have a phone that connects you with the command center. May I use this phone, please?"

The small group of the crew seemed obviously impressed by his polite approach and led Marshall to the telephone. The waiter pushed the button for him.

Someone answered the phone at the other end, but that was as far as politeness went.

"What do you want—to make peace offers, or what?"

"You guessed right, sir. What other reason would I have to talk to you?"

"I have money. And one of the passengers here has a lot of it."

"Thanks a lot for that hint. We'll get the rest of the money sometime during this day. You won't have to worry about that until we are about to land."

"But the money is not here on board, sir. It would make no sense to talk so long here on the phone with you. There are too many people listening in. Will you please give me safe passage to the pilot's section and back again?"

"If you leave your gun behind, you can come here."

Marshall had some difficulties to overcome with the other passengers. Some considered his willingness to negotiate utter nonsense, since he was powerless to do anything in any case. Others expressed open suspicion that he was one of the gangsters, but finally they let him go.

The gangsters received Marshall in the passenger section and brought him to the front. While he walked through the passenger room, he sized up their numerical strength. There were at least ten people who belonged to the gang, which impressed him very much.

The man in the pilot's seat was a well-dressed civilian. With the help of two assistants, he had taken over navigation. He seemed to be quite expert at his job.

"Johnny, take my place as long as I'm talking with this guy here. Well, are you the man that phoned me a little while ago?" he asked Marshall.

Without waiting for an invitation Marshall sat down next to him. "I want to state briefly the way I judge the situation. Then you can make up your mind if I am right or not."

"All right, shoot, little prophet."

"You are after Mr. Adams. You already possess his money. Now you need his life in order to be safe for the future. Since you can't kill him and still land in Tokyo, according to the flight schedule, you plan to land somewhere in south Asia. Then you intend to disappear without being recognized. In this connection, I am very much concerned about the fate of the rest of the passengers, while this hardly seems to worry you. Have I made myself clear so far?"

"Just go on. That wasn't all you had to tell me."

"Yes, that's all to begin with, for my offer makes sense only if my analysis of the situation is correct so far."

"You wanted to get some money for us. Do you know where Adams is still hiding some more? That money is coming from him—isn't that what you mean?"

"Of course. It's a matter of more than 40,000 pounds that he has deposited in a bank in Montreal. I'll sacrifice Adams, with the rest of his money—apart, of course, from some expenses that you'll have to pay to me—but you will guarantee the safety of the rest of the passengers. Is that a deal?"

"How much will your expenses amount to?" asked the boss. Since Marshall had quoted the sum of 40,000 pounds, he suddenly became polite.

"Two thousand pounds. I don't want to take advantage of you."

"That's fair enough. Now, how do we get at that money in Montreal?"

"You'll have to pretend to negotiate with Adams. We'll have to think up some way to allay his suspicions, for in the final solution he is paying his own ransom. I am convinced that he has some code for cabled remittances of money. Using that code, you can swing the deal without any great loss of time. I'll take care of that, sir. He's known me only since this noon, when we met in Croydon, but I have managed to gain his confidence. But now, how about the second part of our bargain? Where are you going to land?"

Marshall was completely concentrating on what the other person was thinking.

"We have a very suitable place somewhere near Rangoon," said the boss, while his thoughts were secretly occupied with an entirely different geographical location. "We can enter negotiations from Rangoon with London, and the rest of your people will have good connections to get another flight from Rangoon to Tokyo."

"Could you tell me what your secret landing site looks like? I am interested in details, because I want to make quite sure."

The boss was thinking of India, and in particular of a region between the Kardamom Mountains and the city of Madura. Characteristic of this region was the transition from a dense jungle into a wide, open savannah grassland.

"This secret airport is an old airport for horizontal thrust engines, but it is quite suitable for our purposes. And we won't run any great risk of being found out. How is it then? Will you talk with Adams?"

"Of course, sir. The best thing will be if I talk to him right away."

"Okay. Go now. Let's consider that we are in a condition of truce."

John Marshall returned to the lounge section. "We will land near Rangoon," he explained to the people. "From there we'll have good connections to Japan or to Korea. The only condition the bandits made was that we remain aboard the plane long enough to give them a good head start. This is the extent of concessions I could get them to make to us."

"You accomplished a good deal if that is true, but not much if we consider that we have no guarantees whatsoever for their promises."

Marshall tried to calm the speaker. "Beggars can't be choosers, sir. If you can obtain better conditions from them, why don't you go and ask them personally?"

Most of the passengers were on Marshall's side and praised his courage.

While the general conversation became more and more animated and while one of the stewardesses announced that they were just flying over the northern Maldives, John Marshall disappeared into one of the washrooms. There he took a small, unusual looking radio transmitter out of his pocket.

"Marshall calling, Marshall calling. I'm calling the Third Power. Please answer. John Marshall calling. Perry Rhodan, please answer."

Inside the blockaded zone of the central Gobi Desert, sirens howled and bells were ringing shrilly.

Reginald Bell's voice boomed over the outdoor loudspeakers of the low lying barracks. "Emergency. Emergency. The emergency squad and all vital personnel, please report immediately to the central compound."

Perry Rhodan, who had just intended to return to the robot brain to have some further detailed calculations made, turned and raced back the 200 yards to the command center. There he arrived at the same time as Kakuta, Captain Klein and Lieutenant Kosnow.

"We have our Secretary of the Treasury," declared Bell, "but he is being held by some bandits inside a big jet that will land in a few minutes at the southernmost tip of west India. Most likely they will kill him at that time. Marshall has just sent this report to me."

"Everybody to the space sphere," ordered Rhodan. "At once!"

Outside he ran into Thora.

"Your fellowmen have another of their alarms," she noted with apparent lack of emotion.

"We need the space sphere, Thora. I hope that neither you nor Khrest planned to use it right now."

"You can have the space sphere, Perry. Evidently this is once again a case of Earth shaking events confronting you."

There was no time for Rhodan to react angrily to her sarcastic remark. He ran on, for the cue words "Secretary of the Treasury" had been sufficient to make clear the significance of this moment.

He had mentally calculated the distance from the Gobi Desert to the tenth degree of latitude, and he had realized at once that he would arrive there too late if he used his special Arkonide suit for transportation. His only hope of crossing the almost 2,500 miles within a few minutes lay with the spaceship.

Exactly eighty-five seconds after the alarm had sounded, the gigantic sphere left the ground. Reginald Bell was reclining in his seat. He had decided not to make use of the automatic guidance system.

"Peter," he called to Kosnow. "Turn the map to west

India. The jet with the bandits will land about ninety miles west of Madura. We must fly toward the jet, a bit toward the south. As soon as we sight it, nothing can go wrong any more. The last time we heard from Marshall, the jet was just above the Maldive Islands."

"Okay," Perry Rhodan said calmly. "We'll make it with this miracle craft. Don't worry."

The Arkonides' sphere flew at an altitude of about eighty miles. Far below, the planet was rotating as if it had been set in motion by a titanic fist. They could see the highlands of Tibet, the Himalayas, Nepal and the Ganges River. For a couple of minutes they were crossing the ocean above the Gulf of Bengal between Jaipur and Madras. Then Reginald Bell sighted the jet. The men gathered eagerly around the video screen.

"You see this glimmering line there? That must be it. They are on a straight course. Altitude approximately 30,000 feet."

"Let's hope they don't recognize us," said Kosnow.

"Impossible," grinned Bell. "We're using our invisible cloak. Even if the people down there looked up straight to the sky above them, they would not be able to make out the slightest suspicious spot. Shall I descend now?"

"Yes," replied Rhodan. "Approach within a mile and a half of them. We'll probably have to land immediately after the jet. I would not like to give these bandits too much time to use countermeasures."

"What could they do against our superior force of arms?"

"There are many hostages on board," Rhodan reminded him. "Under these circumstances our technical superiority will not be of much help to us."

CHAPTER THREE

"What is all this nonsense about 40,000 pounds?" shouted the indignant Homer G. Adams. "I don't have that kind of money. That is a wild pipedream of yours, and even if I had that sum, I would hardly–"

"I know that you don't have that kind of money," Marshall tried to calm him. "But you don't have to tell that to those gangsters. All that matters now is to keep stalling the boss until help from the outside arrives. We must pretend that you possess that amount, and in particular, you must act as if you were ready, willing and able to pay that sum in exchange for your life."

"Until help from the outside arrives?" inquired Adams. "Do you really have that kind of relations that you can speak of such a hope in all seriousness?"

John Marshall grinned mysteriously. "You can think about that for a while. We have exactly three minutes left before we touch down, and then most probably the boss of the gangsters will call you to let him know what you have decided."

Adams looked at his watch and then over to the small screen above the entrance to the ship's galley.

"It's more than 1,200 miles to Rangoon. I think you calculated wrong, Marshall."

"Not at all. We're going to land not far from Madura."

There was no time for further questions; the boss had started the landing maneuvers. The jet descended rapidly, almost like a stone, and all passengers struggled to hold on tight wherever they could. Suddenly there was a hard bump, and the ship came to rest on the ground.

On the screen they could discern a wildly overgrown savannah and in the background the wall of a thick jungle.

Marshall phoned again. When he returned, he declared,

"You are to come along with me, Mr. Adams. All the others must wait until we have concluded our final negotiations. Please, gentlemen, keep calm and as disciplined as you have until now. There is no reason to doubt the favorable outcome of this discussion with the gangsters."

Adams had to use the elevator to reach the front of the jet. The ship now stood vertically, while all the passenger quarters of the plane had turned ninety degrees in their gimbals.

"I want to point out to you," Marshall protested as he entered the command center, "that you have not stood by our agreement so far. Or do you know so little about geography that you can't distinguish between west India and east India?"

"We have changed our minds, Marshall, but this does not change anything regarding our agreement. Madura is not any worse than Rangoon."

"But Madura is at least a hundred miles away from here. How do you expect to get our passengers there within a short time?"

"Just let me worry about that. I am much more interested in what Mr. Adams' attitude is to my proposals."

"Your propositions are, mildly stated, outright blackmail," stated Homer G. Adams angrily. "I have been informed by our friend here what you are demanding from me, and I admit that my life is more valuable to me than any money that I might possess, but I will not pay the ransom until I have obtained valid guarantees for my personal safety from you. Let me know how you plan to proceed."

"It's all very simple. You make out a check for me. I will send it with a messenger to Madura, where I have good connections to a Calicut bank, and then I'll wait to see if the check will clear and if everything is in order. As soon as I have obtained the sum we have agreed upon, I'll let you go, as well as the rest of the passengers."

"That doesn't sound very tempting to me. First of all, it will take much too long, since we will probably lose two full days when you send a messenger to Madura. Second, the mutual guarantees are too one sided, as far as I am concerned. I have no proof whatever that you will release me as soon as you have the money in your possession. Therefore, please think of a better solution and try to be objective about it."

"You obviously misjudge your situation, Mr. Adams," declared the boss cynically. "The advantage is on my side, and I have no intention of giving up my advantage just because you insist on objectivity."

Marshall, whose expression suddenly increased in optimism, interjected, "If anyone is discussing advantageous positions now, it should be *we* and not *you* who can do so. Boss, I suggest that you look at the screen. It might show you a few lovely views of the countryside around us and maybe a few additional surprises."

All the people in the room looked simultaneously at the video screen and saw two odd looking figures that came tumbling down from the sky toward the ground.

"These people are not dressed in divers' suits," added Marshall with satisfaction. "But they are wearing a rather neat technical gadget of a far superior civilization. It is your bad luck, boss, that the men out there are my allies, coming to my assistance. What do you say we give up this fruitless hide and seek game and discuss the real situation? I suggest that you put down your weapons on this table, raise your arms, and then tell us where you have been hiding the regular crew of this plane, so that this jet can still arrive in Tokyo today."

The answer was a burst of insane laughter. On the face of the leader of the bandits, surprise, disbelief, fear and rage played at the same time.

"You are stark, staring mad and imagining things, Marshall. You can't bluff me. Just let these two odd looking characters take a little walk out there. All they probably want to know is why we landed here and not where we were supposed to. I can hardly imagine that they are coming to your rescue. Let's get back to the more important things we were discussing before."

"I must admit, boss, that your carelessness is rather frightening. In your place I would have tried to get rid of such uninvited guests long before now."

"I can't figure you out, Marshall. Sometimes I get the impression that you are trying to join our band. Okay, then, let's shoot. Jim, you take care of that."

Jim rose and reached for a machine gun. He opened a small window and then pulled the trigger, aiming at the two strange men approaching the plane. He kept shooting until the magazine was empty. Then he turned around, wild amazement in his eyes.

"They're still there, boss, and I could bet that at least every third shot was a hit. Does anyone have another magazine?"

"Save yourself that trouble," said a man's voice with a Japanese accent. Only John Marshall seemed to have expected the sudden appearance of Tako Kakuta. The other men turned around and stared with utter confusion at the young Japanese.

"Wh-Who is that?" stuttered the boss. He was so beside himself that it took very little to break any resistance he might have left. The psychoradiator that Tako Kakuta held in his hand was really unnecessary.

"I'm coming as a friend, gentlemen. Put down your weapons over here and then step back against the wall. You are perfectly safe. Nothing will happen to you."

A few seconds later the six disarmed bandits were standing along the wall. They did not resist when Tako put handcuffs on them.

A short while later the rest of the gangster band was overpowered, and the crew of the jet was set free.

John Marshall exchanged a few words with the commanding officer of the jet and wished him a good trip to Tokyo. Everyone was overjoyed that this adventure had taken such a fortunate turn, and they invited Marshall and Tako to a party and asked endless questions.

"I'm sorry to have to disappoint you, ladies and gentlemen, for both Mr. Adams and I will leave the plane here. It is not within my province to give a full explanation of the events of the past hours. Just be happy that you all escaped safe and sound from the hands of these gangsters and that no one was injured in any way."

"I am very much in your debt," said Homer G. Adams to Marshall as he saw the jet disappear above in the clouds. "But of course, I would like to be given some of the explanation you refused to give to the passengers."

"Do you really need any additional explanation?"

"Why not? Do you think I am a telepath?"

"That's something we'll have to find out. In any case, you have been the most successful stock market speculator and financial broker of all time. These things do not happen just by themselves. A supergenius usually possesses a sixth sense. Of course you are endowed with some supernatural talent."

"Do you believe such nonsense? Do you believe in supernatural powers?" inquired Adams.

"No," said Marshall, "for we must separate science from religion. In the one case we know something, and in the other case we only *believe* something. And parapsychology is a science."

"I'm always glad to learn," Adams commented with raised eyebrows. "So far I have been an expert only in money matters."

"This means that you had a good grasp of the psychology of the masses. From psychology to parapsychology is but a step, even if this step leads beyond a wall. You were amazed, for instance, at the sudden appearance of my friend Kakuta. As soon as you look at it with a knowledge of parapsychological matters, you will no longer be surprised at this phenomenon."

"Are you then a parapsychologist?" inquired Adams. He turned to the Japanese. "I must admit that your sudden appearance surprised me even more than that of the gangsters, but I'm sure that in the final analysis we can find a natural explanation for this, too."

"Of course." The Japanese smiled. "If you consider teleportation to be a natural phenomenon, to that extent you are right."

"Tele—what?"

"I am the child of a Japanese couple who were exposed to strong radioactivity after the first American atom bomb at the end of World War II. This caused a mutation of their genes, and as a result of that, I became a mutant."

Homer G. Adams fell silent, and the last trace of irony disappeared from his smile. Finally he said, "If I understand you right, you can change your body into pure energy without the help of any technical means and then rematerialize at any other spot you choose. Did I understand you correctly?"

Tako Kakuta nodded in agreement. "You are right. This is in essence what I can do. The place where I can materialize is subject to rather narrow limits. I might be able to increase the distances slowly if I keep on experimenting."

"That is fantastic, Mr. Kakuta. You, with your phenomenal capacities—" Adams broke off in the middle of his sentence. An important insight seemed to have enlightened him suddenly.

"Go on talking," Marshall urged him. "Kakuta is a very grateful person and is open to any good advice."

"Just a moment, please," Adams demanded. "What was the matter a while ago with our machine gunner? Where did the two men in the strange looking suits disappear to? And why was it not possible to kill them with his machine gun?"

"You're asking a lot of questions all at once. Jim's machine gun fire was ineffective because bullets were absorbed by an energy screen. Nothing has happened to the two men. They have returned to our spaceship, to bring it here. We intend to get out of here as quickly as possible. If I talk with our captain, I'm sure he'll bring you to Tokyo."

"What am I supposed to do in Tokyo, Marshall. I could have continued my flight from there, and then I would have had to change planes once more in Peking. Am I not much closer to my destination here?"

"Here in the savannah at the foot of the Kardamom mountain range?"

"Why aren't we completely frank with each other, Marshall? You had your plans for me ever since we met in London. Isn't it so?"

"That's right. When did you realize this?"

"My brain must have suffered quite a lot during the last fourteen years, but now I can see quite clearly that you are no less stupid than I am. We had both the same goals, but still neither of us knew of the other's intentions."

"That's where you are wrong. I knew about it, all right."

"You knew about my plans? Since when?"

"Ever since you left prison. We were very much interested in you, Mr. Adams. You will understand everything as soon as Mr. Rhodan has informed you of all the details about our unfavorable financial situation."

"And why did you think of me, of all people?"

"You were the first person we should have thought of. You are undoubtedly the greatest financial genius of all time. It is our good fortune that they let you go on living after that sensational trial. Several newspaper reports from the year 1957 came to our attention, and we have studied them, as well as your past, most thoroughly. Rhodan decided to obtain an amnesty for you and to keep an eye on your activities and direct them in such a manner that you would soon find your way to us."

"Just a minute. I was pardoned because of good conduct!"

"You may call it that if you want to. In any case, our agents have speeded up the decision of the Minister of the Interior through Arkonide technical means. We have a psycho-apparatus that influences a person's willingness to make decisions by applying high frequencies. You saw this instrument in action when Kakuta disarmed the gangsters."

"That's all very fine," objected Adams with the last threads of a healthy distrustful attitude. "You have introduced me to a genuine teleporter in the person of Mr. Kakuta. You have demonstrated within a few minutes the most incredible technical facts; but there is still your assertion that you already knew of my plans when I was leaving the prison. It is true that I have read all kinds of newspaper reports dealing with Perry Rhodan during the last week. I have come to admire him, and the desire grew in me to serve this man, if only the opportunity ever arose. But let me tell you that I have not spoken to any living human soul about my intentions."

"But you have thought of them, and that was sufficient for me. . . ."

Once again Adams seemed at a loss for words. The smiling Japanese helped him. "John Marshall is our second 'para.' That explains everything, Mr. Adams. He is a telepath. He knows what is in your mind as long as you think very intently of something."

"This is more than I can take. I'm no youngster any more. You should be a bit more considerate. This is absolutely overwhelming for me."

"If you enter Perry Rhodan's services, you will have to get used to quite a few apparently incredible things. It has been our experience so far that people come to accept these things very quickly. Ah, here are our friends. Let me have your briefcase, please, Mr. Adams."

"That's out of the question. I'm not old enough to need a porter for a few pounds of paper money. By the way, there is one thing that you neglected to explain to me, although in the meantime I found the solution on my own. Didn't the gangster boss tell you that his destination was Rangoon? But nevertheless you knew that he was going to land here. Did you find that out by way of telepathy too?"

"That's right. I was merely bluffing when I was apparently so willing to negotiate with them. All I needed was a brief conversation with the man to determine his real intentions. As soon as I learned that he planned to land west of Madura, all I had to do was inform our friends in the Gobi Desert. They then took care of all the rest."

In the meantime Marshall, Adams and Kakuta were on their way to the Arkonide space sphere. The gigantic ship landed, and the men could make out the figure of Perry Rhodan waiting for them. When they were hardly 500 feet from the ship, Perry Rhodan met them. For the first time, the master of the Third Power and his Secretary of the Treasury faced each other.

"Welcome, Mr. Adams. I'm happy that you have found your way to us."

"It was a very complicated path, Mr. Rhodan, but I was very happy to come to you. I can't stand the lazy life. That was what was most difficult for me to bear during the fourteen years of my confinement. You seem to have some financial worries. Isn't it so?"

CHAPTER FOUR

New York.

Walking north from the corner of Broadway and Fifth Avenue one passes a twenty-two story office building constructed in the early thirties. Its façade is almost completely obstructed by the colorful neon signs of at least a dozen of its tenants. No passerby would even give this ugly array a glance, unless he had some special reason to. It is just like any number of unattractive business buildings in Manhattan.

However, some of the office personnel in the neighboring similarly ugly looking building noticed one sunny Monday morning that a crew of workers had busied themselves on the outside wall between the seventh and ninth stories. The big neon signs for a toothpaste, a hair tonic and an automobile tire were hauled down within a few hours. In their place a huge flashing neon sign was installed that very same evening with just three giant yellow letters, outlined in bright blue: G.C.C. The speed with which the installation of the sign proceeded seemed remarkable and led the attentive observers to make some conclusions about the business mentality of the firm whose huge initials boldly adorned the drab building façade.

What these three giant letters G.C.C. stood for, could be learned the next day from a full page ad in *The New York Times* in which the General Cosmic Co. announced that it had opened its doors for business. They described themselves as consultants and efficiency experts and offered expert advice to any interested parties regardless of their field of business. New sensational manufacturing processes and additional machinery were offered at prices that were really sensationally low, considering the fantastic potential increase in profit.

Homer G. Adams, business manager of the new firm, had hired three young ladies as office help. He was acting on behalf of the firm's proprietor, Benjamin Wilder. He welcomed his help with a pep talk.

". . . the proprietor of our firm has placed me in full charge of these offices. We are a new enterprise without any tradition or predecessors. With your support I hope to gain worldwide recognition for the letters 'G.C.C.' I demand promptness and utmost reliability from you. Whatever special knowledge is required for this type of work you will acquire in a short time, if you apply yourselves. It is to your advantage to be just as young as our firm. We will all grow together, and you have splendid chances for advancement.

"You have here all kinds of business machines for your office work. For the more complicated tasks involving calculation and statistics you see here this tiny electronic instrument. I will shortly instruct you in how it works. Finally, I naturally insist that you make our clients feel welcome in this office. Thank you."

The office hours were from nine to five. At nine-fifteen sharp the first caller arrived. It was a florist's delivery boy with a beautiful bouquet of twenty-four red gladioli. The attached card was signed by Benjamin Wilder, the proprietor of G.C.C. Homer G. Adams smiled pleasantly and made some charming remark to his secretary, Miss Lawrence, about the thoughtfulness of their absent boss. The delivery boy received a generous tip.

As he was leaving he held open the entrance door to a new arrival, who was almost as wide as he was high. He introduced himself as Abraham Weiss to the receptionist, who ushered him in to Homer G. Adam's office.

"Good morning, Mr. Adams. I have read your ad in *The New York Times*. . . ."

"Won't you have a seat, Mr. Weiss!"

Weiss fell heavily back into the wide chair next to Adams's desk and spoke again. "I read your ad, and I decided to find out a bit more about what you have to offer. It seems that you promise quite a lot, you must admit!"

"It all depends on what kind of terms you are used to. What specifically brings you to us?"

"Well, I don't quite know how to begin. My visit here is mainly to obtain information. You know what I mean, of course. I have a fine business, and my motto is live and let live. But I am always curious about any potential improvements, any kind of progress. Could be I might miss some important chance otherwise. That is why I have come to see you."

"Yes, of course. Anyone who fails to take advantage of what G.C.C. has to offer is definitely missing out on a tremendous opportunity."

"That's a wonderful slogan, Mr. Adams. You are so right!"

Although Adams was rather irritated by the way his visitor seemed to beat around the bush, he inquired politely, "How can we be of service to you, Mr. Weiss?"

"Well, my dear Mr. Adams, I have some interests in Colorado. Something that might interest you, too. Do you understand anything about power stations?"

"You mean nuclear power plants?"

"No, hydraulic power. Electricity from a dammed up river. Does that sound too conservative for you?"

"Not at all. So you are constructing a hydraulic power plant?"

"Yes, at the upper Arkansas River, not far from Cripple Creek. But we are not yet constructing it. My firm would be most interested in obtaining that contract, though."

"You are looking for ways of cutting your costs so you may compete in bidding for the contract. Is that it, Mr. Weiss?"

"Not exactly, Mr. Adams. We have already submitted our bid, and I might add that I think we have excellent chances for beating out the other competitors. After all, we are leaders in our field. But just as a matter of principle I would like to know if you have anything up your sleeve that could put us into an even more advantageous position. I just want to get acquainted with you as a future contact. I would like to know what G.C.C. could eventually do for us. On the other hand, I am sure you must be eager to make new contacts, seeing that you are brand new in this field. Any business connections should be valuable to you, particularly with such a reputable house as ours."

Homer G. Adams felt he could do very well without

such gratuitous advice. But he did not let on, especially since he had learned by experience that the braggarts of Mr. Weiss's type were those who needed help most.

"You expressed my own thoughts, Mr. Weiss," he said with a smile, and offered him a cigar. "Please help yourself. I am sure you will enjoy my own private brand."

He waited until his visitor had lit his cigar and was puffing contentedly before he continued, "It would be nonsense to deny that we are trying to get established and therefore appreciate any connections. I am particularly pleased to welcome someone of your stature as my very first customer. But let's go on talking about your project. I admit that hydroelectric power plants are rather on the conservative side, but they are still not out of date. Nuclear power is an important competitor, but in the last analysis, it is all a question of finances. Which is cheaper? And there I would have some tempting suggestions to make to you."

Adams had been observing his visitor intently while he made his long speech. And he had noticed a suspicious twitching in the man's fleshy face. Abraham Weiss slowly abandoned his attiture of feigned indifference, for he definitely wanted more than just to get acquainted with Homer G. Adams.

"Pardon my asking a personal question, Mr. Adams. Judging by the way you talk you must be quite an expert in this special field."

"The construction of power plants is just one of the many fields in which we have specialized knowledge. That is our strong point. You see, people who make claims in newspaper ads, as we did, must be able to back them up with facts. Otherwise, our firm would be doomed right from the start.

"But to come back to your special project, Mr. Weiss. According to my information you have every reason to be concerned about your competitors who made their bids on the basis of nuclear power. The construction of power plants, especially in mountainous areas, is so expensive these days that your chances are none too good. On the other hand, the upkeep of hydraulic power stations is still cheaper today than that of atomic plants. You will win out on your bid if you can manage to build your hydraulic works for approximately the same price as your nuclear competitors."

Abraham Weiss was all eyes and ears. "You are very well informed indeed. But let's go further. You have stated the problem I face. Now let me hear what suggestions you have for a solution!"

Homer G. Adams smiled sweetly. "Such advice is usually not given without charge. Since you are my first visitor and potential client, however, I will throw this much in for free. But in case you should accept my solution, you would need more than just advice. You would also need my machines. First of all I want you to quote me the overall price for the hydroelectric works at Cripple Creek. Then break it down and tell me the cost of the necessary earth movements and getting the terrain ready for construction. Then I will give you my counterproposals."

The fat man sucked on his cigar, obviously deliberating whether he dared quote any actual figures. Then he explained, "I can quote you only proportionate figures. Not real costs. I am not authorized to do so. You see my point, I am sure."

"Why, certainly. Just give me, for example, what proportion of the total cost the earth construction work would comprise."

"Well, let's assume the total cost amounts to 1.3 billion dollars. Then the foundation plus the earthwork would be about 550 million dollars."

"Fine. That gives me enough of an idea, Mr. Weiss. Now let me propose this to you—you purchase my machines, which will lessen the cost of the earth construction work by about ninety percent. That means you can save almost half a billion dollars of the total construction price. Nobody can compete with you on such a basis!"

Abraham Weiss knocked the ashes off his cigar in his excitement and almost burned a hole in his trousers. Then he took a deep breath and forced a smile on his lips. "You certainly have a sense of humor, Mr. Adams. But right now I am more concerned with reality than with such wonderful pipe dreams."

"You are wrong if you think I am joking. I am quite

serious, Mr. Weiss. I do have the machines I was talking about. My firm will be most happy to give you a practical demonstration of them at any time. All you need is to let me know when it will be convenient for you. Provided, of course, that we have first agreed on terms for the deal. For unless you are seriously interested in what we have to offer, we cannot afford such costly demonstrations of our machinery."

Mr. Weiss rose, evidently quite impressed by Adams's words. Adams felt that Weiss must be at a turning point in his business career and that the wily hardheaded businessman must be thinking very hard how to proceed at this point.

Finally Weiss said, "You indicate how I can cut costs by 500 million dollars. But on the other hand I would have to add the purchase price for your machines. How do we stand?"

"You need not worry at all about the purchase price of our machinery in your calculations of the Arkansas River power plant. These machines will be a permanent investment. You can count on twenty to thirty similar construction projects in the future once you own such far superior equipment."

"I see. But please, there must be some price I will have to pay for these machines."

"The price is purely imaginary. That means it would exceed the value of fifty such power plants, if you had to pay cash. Please, let me finish! I don't intend to sell my machinery. Instead, I propose becoming a partner in your firm, Mr. Weiss. This way both of us will be helped."

Abraham Weiss did not take kindly to such a suggestion. "So you are speculating on being my partner?"

"I am not speculating, I am proposing it. That's far more serious, Mr. Weiss. Call a special meeting of your board of directors and tell them to increase your share capital by fifty-one percent. These fifty-one percent will be my price."

Mr. Weiss nervously grabbed his hat and backed toward the door.

"I hope that is not your final offer, Mr. Adams. I could never get my firm to accept these conditions."

"Then I regret having wasted your precious time. My

offer is firm. I am not interested in any financial dealings, unless we can obtain what I quoted—fifty-one percent of your stock, Mr. Weiss. Just give it some thought."

The builder of hydroelectric works bowed slightly and then disappeared through the door leading into the outer office.

The next caller's name was Andre Giletti. His dark hair and wiry figure spoke of his Latin parentage. Miss Lawrence informed her boss that Mr. Giletti had been waiting for forty-five minutes, which led Adams to believe that he, too, must be in a desperate situation.

"Good morning, Mr. Adams," he said politely.

"Hello. How are you, Mr. Giletti? Won't you have a seat here? Cigarette?"

"Thank you, no. I don't smoke."

"You are very fortunate, Mr. Giletti."

"Maybe in this respect, but not in others. Or else I would not have come here."

"You need help? Any technical improvements? Some good advice?"

"All three of them is what I need. And as quickly as possible. I want to get right to the point, Mr. Adams. As soon as you decide that you are not the right man for me, please let me know. The worst thing I could possibly do at this point would be to waste any time."

"Please, start talking! I'll be frank with you."

"I represent the Minneapolis Mining Company. Besides mining we are also interested in constructing big tunnels. You probably know that we are working on the highway between Salt Lake City and San Francisco. Coming from the east we must pierce the Sierra Nevadas for a stretch of about forty-five miles. We have finished excavating a tunnel for about seven miles. But on the opposite side, coming from the west, our competitors have been working faster. They completed a stretch twice as long as we did. There is no doubt that we are going to lose out in this competition."

"I can't share your pessimism! After all, isn't it usual to make arrangements with the government about the deadline you have to meet, regardless of what your competitor might accomplish? Why be upset about that?"

"Let me explain that to you, if you are interested in that kind of thing. By the way, are you familiar with conditions in the mining business?"

"I might say that we pride ourselves in our special knowledge in that particular field. Just go on with your explanations. I am most anxious to hear them."

"Well then, our agreements with the government were concluded for only part and not for the whole project. Each section of the tunnel is treated separately. That means each firm is allocated the next job proportionately to the amount of work they are capable of producing in a given time. Therefore, the government would place only one-fourth of the next order with us, seeing that we can turn out only half as much work as our competitors. Provided, of course, that we can't manage to speed up our output somehow in the immediate future. On the other hand, we have made all our calculations based on the assumption that we would receive exactly half of the job.

"I am sure you will realize that we must make certain dispositions way ahead of time in an enterprise of this nature. We made certain commitments with suppliers of materials and machinery a year ago, and these suppliers will far exceed our needs if we continue working at the same speed. We are financing materials that we will never be able to use. We are paying for that exactly what our profit was supposed to be. And if you add the labor costs for 7,000 workers, we will be completely in the red. This loss will cause us to go into bankruptcy within a few months' time. I am telling you this, Mr. Adams, trusting that you will treat this as a confidential matter. You assured me of utter secrecy in your ad."

"You can depend on us, Mr. Giletti. I am very interested in your problem—almost as if it were already our own, I might add. As I see things, you must bore a large enough hole through this mountain to accommodate a modern freeway. As it happens, I have just taken out the patent for some machinery that could do the trick. What is the size of the tunnel?"

"Twenty feet high and sixty feet wide."

"Excuse me for a moment, plase," said Adams, and began to scribble some quick figures on a piece of paper. Two minutes later his calculations were finished.

"With my special machinery you will be able to advance with your excavation work by a mile and a half daily—provided that you withdraw your own machinery and workers from the area, as long as we use our own patented tools."

Andre Giletti did not protest the way his predecessor, Abraham Weiss, had done, but he seemed quite indignant. "I am in no mood for silly jokes, Mr. Adams. I am fighting for my firm's survival. This is no laughing matter for me. Don't you have anything more realistic to suggest?"

"I was not joking at all, Mr. Giletti. I am ready to give you a quick demonstration of our working methods. Our machines work on the principle of converting matter into pure energy. Of course, not in a spontaneous process as known in the chain reaction of an atom bomb. We control the reaction. We store the energy that is set free during this conversion and sell it later on at a high profit. I am not surprised that you are skeptical. But the General Cosmic Co.'s specialty is radical improvement of current production methods. I strongly urge you to observe how our instrument works. We will give you a sample with one cubic yard of earth. Then after having watched this demonstration you can make up your mind."

"Fine. I hope you will be able to convince us! If what you say is really so it would revolutionize the whole tunnel construction market, and we could make a real killing in it. I can see fantastic possibilities shaping up for my firm. What is your price for the use of your machinery?"

"Fifty-one percent participation in the Minneapolis Mining Co."

Andre Giletti reacted very similarly to Mr. Weiss. He shot out of his seat and stared horrified at Adams, as if he feared for his sanity.

"But that is ridiculous, Mr. Adams! Do you have any idea what kind of firm I represent! We are an enterprise of the first magnitude, and you simply propose to put it into your pocket!"

"My offer is worth more than fifty-one percent of what Minneapolis Mining Co. is worth. You just got through telling me what the fate of your firm would be in another six months, if you continue on your own. But if you decide to accept my offer that would change your moribund enterprise into the world's leader in the construction of tunnels. You should consider me a most unselfish person, if I will be satisfied with only fifty-one percent participation."

Andre Giletti could not hide his trembling hands any longer. "I think I had better leave now, Mr. Adams."

"Please do. I am very pleased to have met you, Mr. Giletti. If you have any more business worries, don't forget to call on me again."

Miss Lawrence announced seven more callers, but none of them represented the grand style of enterprise that would have interested Adams. He got rid of them within a few minutes. He had more urgent matters to attend to.

He placed a long overdue call. "Hello, Klein! What do you have to report about your interview?"

"Mission accomplished! Just two hours ago I happened to run across a reporter from *The New York Times*. We had a couple of drinks together. My anonymity was lifted as if by accident, the way I had planned, and that fellow had to recognize me, of course. You should have seen his expression! He informed me that I was none other than Captain Klein, who had deserted from the U.S. Secret Service, and that the F.B.I. was hot on my trail. I told him that if he was that clever he also ought to know who my new bosses were. And he stated rather naïvely that this was a generally known fact. Then I proposed to him a compromise solution—if he would refrain from revealing my identity and therefore give up the chance for a sensational news item, I would offer him something in exchange, a veritable bombshell. I told him everything about the unknown invaders from space and particularly stressed the point that the world was facing an invasion any moment now. My source of information seemed reliable enough for him. And if he can convince his editor in chief of that bit of news, everyone will be able to read all about it in today's paper."

"Fine! Now it is 11:38 A.M. Go over to the stock exchange now and keep in touch with me. If you should have any doubts then contact me immediately. Dr. Haggard and Dr. Manoli are already at the stock exchange. But make sure not to give away that you know each other. As far as the public is concerned, you are opponents."

Business had been quite calm this morning at the stock exchange. Looking back on the hectic events of the past weeks, this seemed rather welcome. After the sudden establishment of the Third Power in the Gobi Desert the securities market had taken a deep dive. When a third world war appeared imminent, the question was no longer of an economic crisis, but of total collapse. Then various manifestations of Arkonide strength had followed. The political power blocs of the East and the West had forgotten their differences and had formed a world union among all the nations of Earth. The invasion threatening mankind from extraterrestrial enemies had been repulsed by Perry Rhodan. Now the situation in general had improved, and things were looking up again. There was again a rising mood of confidence and hope, which was mirrored in the rising barometer of mankind's state of mind, a high in the stock market.

Now things had returned to normal again, and the hectic weeks were about to be forgotten. It was 11:38 now. By noon the situation underwent a drastic change.

A few minutes earlier Dr. Haggard had offered some oil shares thirty points lower than the market price and had sold them at once. The brokers had simply shaken their heads in surprise and comforted themselves with the thought that some inexperienced amateur was trying to play the stock market with a remarkable lack of judgment. But when the noon editions of the newspaper came out, the brokers were sure that Haggard must have a sixth sense, for he had saved his money just in time.

The panic the brokers experienced on hearing the news of the invasion was not so much fear for their own safety as concern for their money. The din in the hall was tremendous for several minutes, until Mr. Oliver could manage to command their attention via the loudspeaker system.

"Gentlemen, please don't overreact to a mere newspaper report. There is no official confirmation of this rumor. The board will immediately check out the veracity of this article."

He had hardly finished before a gentleman stormed into the hall, shouting loudly that radio Peking had broadcast the same news simultaneously, independently of *The New York Times.*

"Seventy for General Electric!" a voice suddenly shouted. Dead silence fell on the huge room. But then the storm broke loose and quickly grew to hurricane strength. General Electric had opened that morning at 145!

While Mr. Oliver and his ushers, supported by police, were trying desperately to restore order in the big hall, unofficial business deals were being concluded in the corridors. The pessimists were selling frantically while the optimists felt they could make a killing. It took half an hour before Mr. Oliver could control the frenetic buying and selling. There were rumors of closing the stock exchange, but many protested against it.

The G.C.C agents were still holding back. According to their instructions they should wait before starting to buy, even in the present favorable situation. Only when the activity of selling and buying had come to a standstill did Mr. Haggard make a moderate attempt. He caused Standard Oil to drop thirty-five points, and soon pandemonium reigned again. Haggard withdrew quickly and let the others work, until there were more people wanting to buy than to sell. At 12:55 Opiat, Ltd., shares suddenly began to rise.

Homer G. Adams, who had been in constant touch with the events at the stock exchange, spoke a brief order into his microphone. "You have bought Opiat, Manoli. Make a conspicuous private deal with Captain Klein. Go down forty points! After all, everything remains in the same family, nothing can happen to us."

By 12:57 Opiat, Ltd., had lost seventy-five percent of its opening value. The majority of the other securities shortly followed suit. Toward closing time, just as things seemed to have calmed down again, despite the heavy losses the market had sustained, Homer G. Adams dropped his biggest bombshell.

A special radio communiqué announced that an unknown spaceship had lifted a whole fishing fleet several miles up into the air somewhere in the Timor Sea off the northwest coast of Australia. Then all the ships had been dropped again into the water. The newscaster ended his special announcement with these words:

. . . assumptions that these actions emanated from the so-called Third Power must be rejected. After the latest diplomatic negotiations the Third Power must be considered absolutely loyal to the interests of all mankind.

"After the alien spaceship had dropped the fishing fleet back into the ocean, where approximately 400 men lost their lives, the spacecraft was observed to descend again rapidly to almost ground level and open its hatches or air locks, from which several thousands of grotesque looking creatures jumped into the water. They swam around for several minutes and then disappeared under the surface of the ocean.

"There can be no doubt that we are dealing here with strange nonhumanoid creatures whose natural habitat seems to be the ocean. It remains uncertain but most likely that the invasion of the ocean will be followed by an invasion of the land masses. United Nations headquarters has issued its first communiqué that proper steps will be taken against the invaders."

No one was thinking of closing the exchange now! Everyone was frantically trying to sell, at whatever loss. Even the most hardboiled brokers lost their nerve and sold at any price they could get. Within fifteen minutes huge concerns and trusts changed hands. Nobody seemed to wonder that there were still some people risking their money to acquire such worthless enterprises, when the end of the world was coming closer and closer.

The stock market closed. It had experienced the biggest crash in history. The whole world market appeared to have come to a total standstill.

Homer G. Adams sat in his office at G.C.C. in complete silence. He had long since cut off his connection with his middlemen at the stock exchange. He did not want to run the risk of anyone's listening in. He was now enjoying the calm after the storm. He was thinking and waiting.

Toward four o'clock in the afternoon his phone rang. It was Mr. Weiss.

"Hello, Mr. Weiss. How are you?"

"What is your opinion about the situation, Mr. Adams?"

"It's nothing but a joke. Tomorrow everything will have blown over."

"Well, I must say, you are the last optimist in the world."

"That's what I would like to be—the last optimist, the one who laughs last. But I am sure I am not alone. There must be more of my kind. Why are you calling, Mr. Weiss? You wouldn't be interested in my offer?"

"Does the offer still stand?"

"Why, of course. Life goes on, as far as I am concerned."

"Very well, then. I'd like to get together with you tomorrow. I could charter a plane."

"That won't be necessary. We can take mine. It isn't any slower than the fastest plane you could get anywhere in the world."

"Okay, Mr. Adams. Thank you. I'll see you then tomorrow at—"

"Hold it. Have you thought about my terms for our deal?"

"Yes, Mr. Adams. Fifty-one percent for you, as you suggested."

They arranged a meeting for six A.M. the following day.

The only thing that surprised Homer G. Adams about the next business discussion was that he had expected to speak with Mr. Andre Giletti on the phone. Instead the wiry little man called in person at his office.

"Mr. Adams, we have been seriously considering your offer. The Minneapolis Mining Co. agrees to your proposals. We would like you to demonstrate your machines tomorrow morning."

"Tomorrow afternoon, Mr. Giletti. I already have an appointment for the morning in the Midwest. But after lunch I will be able to fly over to Sacremento. Will that suit you?"

"Excellent. This will leave us enough time to clear out the tunnel, so that you can carry out your demonstration without any danger."

"Fine. And you know our terms. I would like to show you the draft of our contract, since you are here in the office already. Then you will need only to sign it tomorrow —we will have it ready for you by then."

Giletti read the agreement attentively. Then he declared, "I agree to all points, except for the percentage of your participation in our enterprise. My partners have authorized me to present this counteroffer to you. They feel it would be too great a disadvantage for us if you had the majority. Therefore, they suggest reducing your share of our stock to forty-five percent."

Adams's face displayed a sweet, fatherly smile. "You act as you did in the good old days, Mr. Giletti. Does it really matter now who controls the majority? Haven't you lost your shirt in today's market crash like everyone else?"

"Not at all, Mr. Adams. You know that our stock has dropped by more than fifty percent. But I am sure that you must still think highly of our company, especially since other shares have fallen far more heavily than ours. You still get a splendid deal by entering our firm, even if you don't control the majority."

"I was called the last optimist on Earth barely half an hour ago. Now I realize that I am not alone in this respect."

The short, dark haired man bowed elegantly and replied, "We understand each other, Mr. Adams. If the Minneapolis Mining Co. can bore tunnels through mountains, then she will become the leading firm for the construction of air raid shelters within the next three days. After that catastrophe in the Timor Sea Down Under, the only money that anyone is willing to spend will be for building underground bunkers. You see how well we are aware of our potentialities in that case. And you will profit from this emergency the same way we will. Of course, it is quite possible that there is a real basis to the current general mood of expecting the end of the world. But if that should be the case, we would have lost everything anyhow. We just prepare for the eventuality that life must go on. And why shouldn't we? Mankind has always managed to muddle along and will continue to do so as long as any human being is alive."

Homer G. Adams seemed impressed by such a high opinion of humanity's potential for survival. "All right, then. I'll have the contracts typed out and will bring them along with me when we meet tomorrow. G.C.C. will be satisfied under the circumstances with forty-five percent. We will get along with each other."

Two days had gone by.

The demonstrations of the work capacity of General

Cosmic Co.'s machinery had been completed successfully, and the contracts had been signed. Homer G. Adams had flown to the central Gobi Desert base of the Third Power to report on his activities of the last few days. Even Thora and Khrest, who normally preferred not to participate in intraterrestrial affairs, came to listen to Adam's report.

"What is the state of mind of the people on the outside?" inquired Rhodan.

Homer G. Adams lowered his huge head for a moment and then looked around at his friends. "The events of the past days seem to be a repetition of previous experiences that I have gone through. But at that time I was put behind bars for it. This time around, I realize that my actions can be justified. But I want to emphasize that I do not feel responsible for the suicides committed. If they can't get over the loss of material possessions, well, it's their own affair. Besides, I believe that most suicides were caused by the fear of the threatened invasion."

Adams looked over at Reginald Bell while Rhodan said, "Whichever way you look at it, we can't deny having caused mankind a great deal of anxiety. All in this room here know, however, that our action is justifiable, for the invasion is a real threat, not just an imaginary one. The alien invader fleet might arrive any day, any hour. The horrible 3-D film that Bell projected over the Timor Sea with the fantastic Arkonide instruments might possibly have been a preview of what lies in store for all of us on Earth. We have the duty to protect the human race from such dangers, for we alone are powerful enough to do so. This, on the other hand, leads to our obligation to reinforce our industrial potential, which again is possible only if we exert sufficient influence over the world's economy. A constitution that is supposed to unite and protect a planet must necessarily also control its economic potential. Last week, when you went to New York, we had only modest financial assets. What is the situation now, Mr. Adams?"

"Mr. Bell's Arkonide spectacle over the Timor Sea has tipped the scales for us. We have already laid some solid groundwork, though. We managed to bring utter confusion to the New York Stock Exchange, the same as Mr. Kakuta in Tokyo, Mr. Marshall in Cape Town, Mr. Li Tschai-tung in London, and Mr. Kosnow in Berlin. With a comparatively ridiculous sum of a few million dollars we have bought up whole industries and attained majority in four major concerns. Naturally, it won't be possible to give repeat performances of this financial coup, for the world does not fall twice for the same trick. Besides, such tactics would be irresponsible. We don't want to destroy the world economy. Yesterday's maneuver can happen only once every thirty years. It takes a long period of recovery after any major bank crash. If a second should follow too soon, we might face a total collapse of the world economy. We want to avoid that at all costs, because we, too, would suffer by it. We don't want to buried under the ruins of a destroyed economic system. Believe me, gentlemen, I have a great deal of experience in this field. We have gone as far as possible but we have reached the limits now. Is there anyone here who does not agree with me?"

Homer G. Adams's glance swept the round of the assembled group. His question was directed to all of them, but everyone knew that it was really meant for Rhodan alone. "Your success has borne out our prophecy, Mr. Adams," declared Perry Rhodan. "You will remember my initial skepticism. I would have settled for less than you produced. The way things stand now, I must express my sincere gratitude and admiration for what you accomplished for the Third Power. In addition, you have arranged some advantageous business deals with our Arkonide machinery. Still, it seems advisable now to proceed a bit more cautiously."

"Why, of course. We will always take into consideration Khrest's veto power. And you, Mr. Rhodan, always have final say in what the public is permitted to learn of the secrets of the Arkonide technology. The energy matter converter that I put at the disposal of the Minneapolis Mining Co. and Mr. Weiss of the Steel and Concrete, Inc., is already an obsolete model by Arkonide standards. But they were most helpful to us in our present situation. Both firms in which you hold the majority under the fictitious name of Benjamin Wilder as proprietor of G.C.C., have already outpaced any competitors in their special fields; they will be the leaders in the economic revival that will follow the current financial crash. I cannot foresee any financial difficulties ahead for us. We can pay off immediately the seven billion dollars to the Peking government for the purchase of our territory. We will no longer need to make the payments in several installments the way we had planned. It is now all cash on the line. In addition to that we will have at our disposal another four billion dollars within the next six weeks or so, which we will use for our assembly plant inside our domain."

Rhodan seemed pleased with Adams's report. "We have accomplished a lot these past few days," he commented. "There is still a great deal more to be done. We now have the financial means that we so urgently needed. Whatever else we require will be provided through Mr. Adams's financial wizardry. Although we can't count on another bonanza as the last stock market crash, we will find ways to acquire interests in big industrial concerns, with the help of the superior Arkonide machinery, exactly the way we did with Mr. Weiss's and Mr. Giletti's firms.

"But this is really the least of my worries. It will be months or even years before we can build up an efficient industrial program inside the realm of the Third Power. On the other hand, we are facing burning problems that must be dealt with at once. The Fantan invasion might occur any day now. Reg's most convincing trick film could become the reality of tomorrow. Then, however, the hostile invaders won't simply disappear into the waters of the ocean, never to be seen again!

"Another immediate problem is our lack of human resources for the Third Power. The Arkonide robots will not be able to provide all the help we must have in the near future. We need collaborators, living beings and not machines, who will watch out for our interests all over the globe. I will issue further instructions in this regard later on in the day. But for the moment, let me say this—whoever brings a new citizen to the domain of the Third Power will have to be one hundred percent sure of his worth and usefulness for us. Considering our limited space, we can accommodate only a limited number of these collaborators in our new state. Since we are forced to make tremendous demands on each of the new people, we can accept only the cream of the crop of mankind to join us here in our endeavors. We must search for persons with new faculties!"

"You mean, we must find mutants, positive mutants," commented Bell.

Rhodan replied with a silent nod. He did not speak of the vision that Bell's words had conjured up in his mind. Instead he posed a seemingly unconnected question to Adams. "Say, Adams, what is the cube of 2,369.7?"

The short man looked perplexed and then picked up his slide rule.

"Not that way!" interjected Rhodan. "Calculate in your head."

"That will take a little while. . . ."

"Well then, forget it! The result is 13,306,998,429.873. By the way, I am puzzled about one thing you mentioned earlier in our conversation. You talked about our having acquired the majority in the firms of Steel and Concrete, Inc., as well as the Minneapolis Mining Co. But in the beginning you stated that only Mr. Weiss would accept the fifty-one percent clause while Mr. Giletti concluded the bargain with you at only forty-five percent."

"Oh, that's quite simple," explained Adams. "We had previously purchased seven percent of the Minneapolis Mining shares on the stock market. Of course, Giletti had no idea of that when he came to me to seal the deal."

Perry Rhodan waited until the general laughter had abated before he continued, "Wonderful! Congratulations on your accomplishments! But now let us discuss the details of our next enterprise—roundup of the mutant corps!."

CHAPTER FIVE

Colonel Kaats had sent some alarming news from New York to the Greenland base of Allan D. Mercant, who was overwhelmed with pressing work and had therefore only reluctantly flown to see the colonel. Mercant blew his top when Kaats's urgent affair turned out to be nothing but a report of the disappearance of the mutant Anne Sloane. She had been ordered to work in east Asia, where her special telekinetic abilities were needed by the Secret Service of the Western Bloc. Now no trace of her could be found.

"You make me fly here, almost 3,000 miles to New York, just to tell me that, Kaats?"

"I had to talk with you, Mercant. Isn't that sufficient? Isn't a secret agent important enough, if we are dealing with an irreplaceable mutant?"

"You mean to say if that agent happens to work for the inner defense and federal criminal police, Kaats," corrected Mercant angrily. "Let me tell you something, Kaats! Just don't bother about Anne Sloane for one full month. If she is supposed to find out something for us, then we must allow sufficient time for her to do the job. She might be a para, all right, but she is still very immature and knows little of what it's all about in this life. I had advised her to proceed cautiously rather than act rashly. After all, she is just an amateur at this game. And now, Kaats, I hope you don't mind if I leave you in a hurry. I am drowning in work at the Greenland base."

"Come on, first have a drink with me!" Kaats insisted amiably. "I can't let you leave in such a horrible mood."

Mercant had his glass of whiskey. "You know, Kaats, the only thing that made my flight to New York worthwhile is the excellent whiskey here. But please, avoid such false alarms in the future! I hate such waste of my precious time!"

Mercant was still angry as his jet descended to land at the airstrip at Umanak Fjord. The most infuriating thing about this whole trip to the United States was his own lack of secrecy. He should never have shared his private opinion about Anne Sloane with Colonel Kaats. Anne was a delicate young girl and totally unfit for secret service work. True enough, he had urged her himself to accept the job, but now he had definitely changed his mind.

In a short while he made his way to the bungalow on which the name of the fictitious firm UMANAK FUR COM-

PANY could be read in huge letters. It was not an outright lie, for the secret service center really did deal occasionally in furs for more efficient camouflage of its real activities.

Mercant descended in the elevator down to the fifteenth floor. There he transferred to another elevator, since no direct connection existed between ground level and the main quarters of the secret service, for security reasons. Down below, at a depth of nearly two miles, lay Mercant's realm. The guards at the doors and in the hallways saluted smartly at his approach. Hardly ten persons of all the five hundred people working at the base had been initiated into the secret installations of this underground maze. These ten were the only ones permitted to move freely without presenting their identification papers.

Mercant had to cross three rooms before he reached his own office. There he sank with a sigh into a deep armchair and settled down comfortably.

Then he rang for his orderly. Almost immediately Sergeant O'Healy responded to his summons.

"Anything special happen while I was away, Sergeant?"

"No, sir!"

"Thank you. What is the time?"

"Seventeen minutes past eleven, sir."

Mercant was satisfied. He had made sure that it was just sixteen minutes past eleven. "What time of the day is it?"

"Morning, sir."

That meant it was night, and with these wrong answers the true identity of Sergeant O'Healy had been sufficiently established.

"All right, Sergeant. Tell Captain Zimmerman that I'd like to see him!"

"Captain Zimmerman is not on the base at the moment, sir. He is on a routine patrol flight."

"Hmm. Does he still believe that our enemies are going to creep up on us across Greenland's icy desert, while the agents of other secret services keep bumping into each other right here on the base?"

"I wouldn't know what Captain Zimmerman believes, sir."

"Well, I am going to find that out for myself. I want

him to report here in my office within ten minutes. Call him on the radio!"

"Yes, sir."

O'Healy disappeared but came back shortly. "I spoke with Captain Zimmerman and relayed your message to him. Captain Zimmerman said that he might be a bit delayed. He just made a strange discovery and wants to investigate it further before reporting back to you."

"What kind of a discovery is that?" asked Mercant in a brusque tone.

"He could not tell. Evidently he did not know himself what he had encountered."

Mercant dismissed the sergeant. Then he pulled out the bottom drawer of his writing desk and switched on the built in radio transmitter. O'Healy's report had been too skimpy; therefore, Mercant preferred to get in touch directly with Captain Zimmerman.

"Calling Captain Zimmerman! Come in, Captain Zimmerman! Mercant calling Captain Zimmerman!"

Mercant waited in vain for a reply for almost ten seconds. Then he heard Zimmerman's voice. He had obvious difficulty speaking. He started with a low moan. "Hello, this is Captain Zimmerman, sir. I must have blacked out for a moment. My head is swimming, and I am seeing spots in front of my eyes."

"What has happened, Captain Zimmerman?"

"I don't know myself. I am returning to base at once, sir."

"What is your location? I am sending another plane to escort you back here."

"That won't be necessary, sir. I'll make it with the help of the autopilot."

"Are you sure? Call if you need any help, will you!"

"Certainly, sir. Thank you."

Mercant switched off and then called the airfield. "Captain Zimmerman seems to be in difficulties. Let me know his present location. You have his flight plan, don't you?"

A short time later Mercant was informed that Zimmerman was just flying over the northern coast near Proeven and was flying south by southwest. Apparently he had regained full control over his machine.

Captain Zimmerman made an uneventful landing, then went directly down to Mercant's private office.

"I am sorry to be late, sir," he said. "I must have run into some unusual turbulence, which apparently caused a rapid drop of the plane. Anyhow, the unexpected acceleration seems to have made my head snap back suddenly and bumped it against the ceiling of the cabin. I must have lost consciousness for a few moments."

"Let me see your head!"

Mercant inspected the wound. "That doesn't look too good, Captain. You will have to get medical attention for it right away. But before you leave, tell me about the mysterious discovery you mentioned to Sergeant O'Healy."

As Mercant made these comments, he was almost overwhelmed by shock. Looking at the wound, he had stepped immediately behind Zimmerman. There he picked up a thought impression with the help of his rather feeble telepathic powers. This thought frightened him thoroughly. Fortunately, Mercant was endowed with outstanding presence of mind. Any man who had worked up his way to the leading figure in the International Intelligence Agency within a few short years must be blessed with very fast reactions.

He had just begun to suggest that Zimmerman seek medical attention, when he became aware of the deadly thought. He managed to complete his remarks without any apparent interruption.

"What discovery, sir? Oh, that was just a joke!"

"You mean to say you were taking the liberty of playing jokes on me?" asked Mercant sharply. He was still standing behind the captain, who was seated in a chair. Mercant did not have the slightest intention of abandoning this advantageous position.

"That joke was intended for Sergeant O'Healy. I had no idea that he would report this to you."

"Very odd, Zimmerman, what strange notions you suddenly develop about our regulations here on the base. On the one hand you go out on patrol flights for the protection of our center, and on the other hand you indulge in silly jokes. This seems rather incompatible to me. Well then, tell me what you saw out there."

"Nothing, sir."

"Remain seated, Captain!" commanded Mercant as Zimmerman began to stand up.

Mercant was fighting to achieve utmost concentration. Several weeks ago he had read in the newspapers about an Australian bank teller who had foiled some bank robbers thanks to his telepathic powers. For quite some time Mercant had noticed similar abilities in himself. He had finally realized what it meant that he was capable of reading someone else's mind, so to speak, during critical moments. He would have given anything now to be a genuine telepath! He was nothing but a clumsy amateur in this field. He was unable to comprehend clearly the other person's thought. He could not discern word by word, but only get a general impression of thoughts.

How was it possible to avoid misunderstandings? Why should Zimmerman be thinking of killing him? There was murder on Zimmerman's mind, though, quite unmistakably. This murderous desire was concentrated on the Chief of the International Intelligence Agency. That meant him—Allan D. Mercant! He had become absolutely sure of this now.

Mercant glanced over Zimmerman's shoulder and saw his gun in the holster. For a split second he pondered taking possession of it by a surprise move, but he quickly dismissed the idea. Zimmerman, his mind preoccupied with the intention of killing Mercant, was already concentrating on his weapon and would beat the physically inferior Mercant to it. Mercant had to get to his own gun now—the one in the bottom drawer of his writing desk just next to the radio transmitter.

If both were equally armed, Mercant would have the advantage, for the captain had not the least inkling that his intended victim was forewarned. To bring about this situation would involve a great risk for about five to six seconds, since Mercant had to leave his sheltered place behind Zimmerman to reach his writing desk. Mercant's ruse was the skillful use of words, which made his adversary curious and caused him to hesitate in anticipation.

"Wait a minute, Captain Zimmerman. I listened in to your radio conversation with Sergeant O'Healy and taped it. Something was said there that puzzled me, and you might supply an explanation. I was not under the impression that you were merely joking. Or how would you explain the following matter? . . ."

"What do you mean by that?"

Mercant started his dangerous walk around the writing desk. Zimmerman turned with his swivel chair, following Mercant with his eyes. Finally both men sat facing each other, the huge desk between them. Curiosity had won out in Zimmerman. He did not shoot; he waited.

Mercant opened the desk drawer and switched on the tape recorder. At the same time he grasped his gun. At once he felt safe again. He turned the tape recorder off.

Zimmerman flared up. "Why did you stop? Why don't you play the tape? No secrecy all of a sudden, sir!"

"Patience, patience, Zimmerman! Just a question before I start playing that tape—what advantage do you expect if you kill me?"

This question brought about the end of their conversation. Zimmerman was too startled by the unexpected turn in their talk to maintain total control over his body. The would-be assassin knew he had been found out, but he still wanted to execute his plan.

He tore his gun from the holster, but before he could aim and shoot, he had lost valuable time. Mercant's weapon had been pointed at Zimmerman through the knee opening in his desk. Mercant simply pulled the trigger while the assailant was still trying to get into position.

The captain collapsed like an empty sack. He was dead before he could cock his pistol.

An unprecedented event in the history of the Greenland base of the International Intelligence Agency followed—Sergeant O'Healy stormed into Mercant's private office without having been summoned! He was wildly waving his gun, but he stopped in his tracks when he saw the unharmed colonel sitting in his chair. Wild eyed, he stared at the dead man in the chair in front of the desk.

"Sir, what has happened here?"

"I shot Captain Zimmerman. Give the general alarm! I'll give the orders myself for sealing off the buildings."

O'Healy saluted and disappeared. Shortly thereafter the sirens began howling on all floors of the underground installations.

Mercant went to the intercom and spoke over the public address system. "Mercant speaking. Calling all personnel. We are in a state of emergency from this moment on! Officer of the Guard, Lieutenant Houseman—blockade all exits! Special surveillance of all elevator shafts. All other personnel to go immediately to their work stations or private quarters. Members of foreign delegations please assemble in the transfer hotel on the top floor. Await further instructions there. Explanations will follow later. Colonel Cretcher and Dr. Curtis are to report at once to my office. Thank you."

The colonel and the physician arrived almost simultaneously at Mercant's private office. Dr. Curtis stepped over to Zimmerman's body.

"Please, Dr. Curtis, examine him at once and tell me if he is dead."

"Do you need any confirmation for that, Mr. Mercant?"

"Yes, for the sake of formality."

"Killing a person is not a matter of formality, sir," protested Cretcher. "Why did you shoot him?"

"To prevent him from shooting me first."

"You mean to say that Captain Zimmerman attacked you? Pardon me, sir, for being so blunt. Do you have any eyewitnesses that can confirm you acted in self-defense?"

"You will forgive me for being equally frank, Cretcher. You have no business accusing me here. I called you to help me clear up many problems that pose themselves in this situation. I know very little about the scene that just took place here in this room. All I can tell you is that he wanted to kill me and I prevented him from doing so by shooting him. These are the facts. But I must learn the reasons that led one of our most trustworthy people to such an attack on my person. Zimmerman's action seems so absurd that we must consider the possibility of a plot. That is why I have declared a state of emergency. We must proceed swiftly in case there should be any accomplices of Zimmerman's on the base who have been plotting against myself and our headquarters."

Mercant turned to the doctor. "You have noted that Zimmerman is dead, Dr. Curtis. There is no doubt what led to his demise. Nevertheless, I would like you to examine Zimmerman's head. I have noticed there a very conspicuous wound. The captain gave me a rather odd reason how he obtained it."

Curtis examined the wound and stated, "Somebody must have struck a violent blow against Zimmerman's skull, from above. But how is this possible? You told me yourself that you shot him."

"How do you mean that?"

"You shot him dead—you did not strike him dead!"

"How old is his head wound, Doctor?"

"Approximately half an hour."

"But half an hour ago Captain Zimmerman was still outside the base flying on patrol. There are plenty of witnesses for that."

"I can't understand all this," the doctor said. "Didn't Zimmerman show any signs of weakness? No, all signs point to it that the blow to his head was fatal. He was killed when something or someone struck him on the skull."

"You must be mistaken. Zimmerman was very much alive when he came to my office. But be that as it may, I am very much intrigued by your diagnosis. I would be interested in finding out how and where the captain was killed for the first time and how he managed to live on despite his fatal wound. Let's inspect his airplane. Would you please accompany me upstairs to the airfield!"

The machine was a four seater, so Mercant, Curtis and Cretcher could sit down in it without being cramped.

"Here is the pilot's seat," said the chief, and sat down in it. "The captain claimed that he had encountered some turbulence and had descended rapidly when he hit an air pocket. This caused excessive acceleration, which snapped his head backward. Now, gentlemen, could you explain to me where he might have hit his head?"

The answer was obvious. Zimmerman had lied. Seat number three had been behind him. He would have had to stand up to hit his head against the cabin ceiling.

"Besides, we should see some bloodstains on the ceiling," said Cretcher.

Mercant inquired from the officer on duty, "Which plane did Captain Zimmerman fly today on his patrol mission?"

"This one, sir."

"Thank you." Then Mercant addressed his two companions.

"Make yourselves comfortable in your seats, gentlemen. We will retrace Captain Zimmerman's patrol flight."

Mercant started the engine and flew along the coastline in a northerly direction.

"Captain Zimmerman acted rather unusual during his mission," remarked the chief. "When I ordered him to return to base he spoke of some strange discovery he had just made. He wanted to investigate it still further. Then he did not reply for quite some time and then claimed to have lost consciousness for a while. The whole affair must have occurred north of Proeven."

Mercant descended to 2,500 feet after having flown over Proeven. He asked his companions to participate actively in optical observation of the terrain.

The weather was clear, and there was no wind. If Zimmerman had noticed something, then it must still be visible barely an hour later. Cretcher called out suddenly, "Down there! Do you see it? There are some landing tracks . . . that must have been made by Zimmerman's machine . . . and then next to them . . . this round spot! What on Earth can that be?"

Mercant turned around and flew once more over the site. He descended to 300 feet. They could clearly distinguish now that the round spot was really a hemisphere something like an igloo but completely black. They could recognize the landing tracks very distinctly. There was no doubt that Zimmerman's plane had made them.

They landed close to the black "igloo." Mercant stepped out and reached it first. He touched it. "Odd! It's made of metal. Who would construct such a funny looking thing in the middle of nowhere here in the Arctic? And it doesn't even have any entrance or windows. I can't find any welded seams, either. What do you think of that, Cretcher?"

"It looks like nothing I have ever encountered. Almost unEarthly!"

Mercant knocked on the unknown material that he had called metal. There was a hollow sound.

Mercant knocked on it once more.

"Step back, gentlemen! I can't locate any door or any other opening, but we will get inside it somehow. I want to know for sure what we are dealing with."

The men stepped back and opened a concentrated barrage on the igloo with their machine guns. But the bullets could not even dent the metal of the strange structure.

"Wait a moment. I'll get some explosives from the plane."

Their efforts were crowned with success. The force of the explosion lifted the hemisphere up, which caused it to topple over. Underneath it they saw a small crater that the detonation had hollowed out in the snow . . . and a torn body. This body was naked and hairy but of an undefined nature. Curtis picked up a limb that might have been an arm but unlike any arm they had ever seen on any living being on Earth.

"Six joints," murmured Dr. Curtis with fascination. "This creature must have come from another world. Unfortunately it is dead, and we cannot reconstruct its original shape. But it is certain that this is what Captain Zimmerman encountered when he landed here on his patrol flight. What are you going to do now, sir?"

"Just gather up all the pieces, and we'll take them along with us. I'm afraid that Rhodan doesn't know anything of this monster! He will be interested in it all the more. I have an idea that this is the start of the invasion that has frightened mankind for days and weeks with nightmarish dreams!"

CHAPTER SIX

Nagasaki, Japan.

More than 40,000 spectators had gathered at the Kashiri stadium to watch the final game of the Japanese Football League. The air was oppressive and filled with the tense mood of the crowd, eagerly awaiting the outcome of the game.

Two men were sitting in Section F of the huge arena. In their pockets was hidden some complicated machinery. Although they were separated by more than 150 feet, the two remained in constant communication with each other. The brainwave location finders functioned smoothly and almost noiselessly. The instruments' slight hum was completely drowned out by 40,000 roaring voices.

Tako Kakuta and Reginald Bell were not really interested in what was going on down on the field. They merely pretended interest by visually following the football, since they did not want to arouse suspicion. All their thoughts were concentrated on their real mission—hunting for mutants to swell the ranks of Rhodan's small troop of faithfuls.

Their miniature radios were masterpieces of precision tooling. The transmitters were constructed of two tiny plastic foils, lying on top of each other. In the space between them were arranged all the technical elements. They wore the senders attached to the inside of their shirt collars, which also hid the highly sensitive throat microphones capable of picking up the slightest whisper. The men had hidden the receivers in their ears, where they took up as much space as a small cotton ball.

Suddenly Bell received a message from Kakuta. "Abnormal brainwave pattern. Most remarkable superimposed waves at 33,000 angstroms. What do you make of it?"

"Incredibly high value, Tako. Even considering the excitement of this football match, such a high frequency is totally outside the normal range. Do you have the coordinates for the man's seat?"

"I have them marked down."

"All right. Wait until I have him located too."

Reginald Bell was working with one hand in his pocket. The direction finder's antenna swept along the rows of spectators in their seats of Section F. Since Bell knew the value of the abnormality he was searching for, it was almost child's play for him. He receiver settled automatically as soon as it hit the target it was looking for.

"These are my coordinates, Tako. According to the seating plan it is 135 degrees, seven minutes, thirty seconds."

"Thanks! My readings are forty-six degrees, twelve minutes exactly. Please calculate the exact location of the man's seat."

Both Tako and Bell were busy calculating for a moment.

Then they compared their results. The seat was number 844 in Section F.

"That's perfect!" said Bell. "I am going now to the main entrance. It's another twenty-five minutes till half-time."

"Very good," replied Tako. "Take care of the robot commando."

The plan of action had been worked out in detail and to perfection. With the help of Arkonide instruments they had determined from some distance away where their mutant target was. But to be on the safe side Tako wanted to have a quick look at his compatriot from close by.

He approached his seat in an inconspicuous manner and snapped a picture of the pleasant faced twenty-five year old fellow. Then Tako made his way up the stairs. There near the entrance he met Reginald Bell.

"Everything went fine. Here is a photo of the young man. Are the robots ready for action?"

Bell nodded briefly and then put the picture into his pocket. Both waited for the end of the game, when the people would be leaving their seats. Then the two mutant hunters would close in on their prey.

Tako and Bell stationed themselves at opposite ends of row 34. The young man from seat 844 walked toward the right, where Bell would have to intercept him. But the suspected mutant was in the company of two friends. Rhodan's emissaries would have to exercise some patience.

Outside the stadium the robot car was parked amid thousands of other automobiles. The robot's direction finder was already set for the young mutant Japanese, who was getting into his car quite some distance away. His two friends were riding with him. The traffic was too thick to get anywhere near the trio's car. Bell and Tako had to rely entirely on their brainwave direction finder to maintain contact with their intended catch.

Bell and Tako communicated via their miniature radios. Kakuta managed to push his way toward Bell but did not quite reach him.

"Do you see that dark red car over there? That's the one!"

"Impossible to get to it. And the robots are parked too

far in the back of the lot. Take your car, Bell. That's the best solution now."

"But those guys will have disappeared before I even can get my car started!"

"Just a moment! Make a right turn—that's a shortcut to the freeway. This way you can overtake the dark red car. Keep close to it; don't lose it from your sight!"

"And how about you, Tako?"

"I'll take a taxi."

"But that's nonsense! You will lose too much time that way!"

Tako smiled. "Don't worry about that. I'll make up for the lost time. Just keep in touch with me!"

Several hundred yards behind him followed the robot car, which remained inconspicuous because of its polarized glass panes, which prevented anyone from seeing what was inside.

Tako seemed to have got the worst of the bargain. His taxicab was hemmed in by the traffic and could advance only very slowly. Tako kept urging the cab driver on, but the cab was solidly caught in the traffic jam.

After fifteen minutes of snail paced progress Tako realized that something had to be done; he would have to act very quickly.

"They have just stopped their car," reported Bell via radio. "I just drove past them. They probably want to go to a restaurant. There is one at the corner of the next big intersection."

"I know the place," confirmed Tako. "Turn around. We will meet in the restaurant. Relay instructions to the robot car to keep an eye on the dark red automobile and to park somewhere near it."

Tako was aware that it would take him at least another fifteen minutes by taxi to reach the corner where the others had stopped. He decided to act. No longer did he urge the taxi driver to hurry up but quietly placed the amount of his fare plus a generous tip on the back seat. Then he concentrated on teleporting himself into the washroom of the corner restaurant.

The cab driver probably wondered for the rest of his life where his passenger had gone. But what really mattered to him was that he had not been cheated out of his fare.

Kakuta's body passed into a state of pure energy and then rematerialized at the destination he had been concentrating on. He arrived at the restroom the same instant that the man from seat 844 was entering the restaurant with his friends. It was not difficult for Tako to get a table close to that occupied by the trio. And when Reginald Bell finally made his way into the dining room, the greater part of their difficulties had been overcome.

"We got him!" said Bell jubilantly. "Let's drink to that!"

They enjoyed their drink. Waiting was not an unpleasant task under the circumstances. The rest of their plan would be carried out by their robots.

Three hours later the three friends left, and each went his own way to return to their nearby homes. The mutant lived around the corner from the restaurant. The plate at his front door carried the name TAMA YOKIDA.

Later in the evening someone rang his doorbell. Tama Yokida answered the door, not expecting anything unusual, but his suspicions were aroused by a strange hissing sound. That was the last conscious thought he had, for he had already breathed in a large dose of a fast acting anesthetic gas spray. Two shadowy figures of plastic and metal carried him swiftly to a car parked in front, which sped away into the dark night.

While the robot commandos were abducting the mutant Tama Yokida in a style devoid of any personal element, Reginald Bell and Tako Kakuta were already out tracing down further suitable candidates for the Third Power. For the finale of their action in Japan they had purchased two expensive tickets for the Metropole Opera House and had arrived at their loge seats for the evening performance.

When the first intermission came around they had already detected three persons in the audience with abnormal brainwave patterns. Security permitted them to deal with only one subject at a time. Therefore, they chose as their target the person showing the strongest deviation from the norm of human brainwave patterns.

The suspected mutant in the audience was a single girl by the name of Ishi Matsu. A gentleman friend accompanied her home. He had hardly left her at her front door before the robot commando rang the bell. Thinking her escort had returned for some reason, she opened the door. She was carried off shortly before midnight.

In the meantime Bell and Kakuta were sitting in their hotel room, having a few drinks and discussing the results of their campaign.

"Twelve mutants. Rhodan will be very pleased. He asked for only ten. Let's quickly check the list again. André Noir, son of a French couple residing in Japan; Ralf Marten, son of a German father and a Japanese mother. The rest of the group all Japanese citizens. Ishi Matsu the only woman among them. The men: Wuriu Sengu, Son Okura, Tanaka Seiko, Doitsu Ataka, Kitai Ishibashi, Nomo Yatuhin, Tama Yokida."

"That makes ten altogether."

"Of course. In addition to these we have Fellmer Lloyd, who is our proof that mutations are not solely due to atom bomb explosions. The same as with Ras Tschubai, whom we found in Africa. That makes a round dozen."

"Are you superstitious?" asked Tako suddenly.

"Why?"

"I am still thinking of our thirteenth mutant. We have another two days to go. . . ." With these words Tako pointed to a newspaper clipping on the table.

"Oh, that story about the German from Munich. I don't believe there is any truth to that report," countered Bell.

"Shouldn't we reserve our judgment until we have personally checked into the matter? Of course, it's an old trick to draw attention to yourself by making all kind of prophecies for the future and having some eager reporter write an article about it in the papers. But appearances indicate that Ellert tried his best to avoid any publicity for his predictions. One of his friends supplied the information to one of the local newspapers. *Teletemporation* . . . I can see all kinds of new possibilities for us with Ellert's special gift. I am greatly intrigued by this so far hypothetical aberration. But if it should turn out to be true . . . ! And besides, he would be the only one we would not have to kidnap. It seems he is trying to join Rhodan in the Gobi Desert base."

"Well, we should certainly help him to get there, if he wants to!"

CHAPTER SEVEN

As the first rays of the rising sun were reflected by the mirrorlike surface of the Goshun Salt Lake in the Gobi Desert, no one could have known what tremendous events the young day held in store for all mankind. Originally Rhodan had intended to inspect the progress being made in the construction of their finishing plants. The first prefab parts had just arrived from Pittsburgh, and the work robots had erected the huge assembly sheds within the past three days.

Perry Rhodan stepped from his personal bungalow, which stood not far from the two spaceships. His attention was drawn to a strange scene. He quickly changed his original plans and observed a group of four people who came toward him, calling and waving. He stood there waiting for them to come closer. He could distinguish now a female figure among the group. She seemed to follow the men rather reluctantly.

Anne Sloane was near collapse. Clumsily, she took a photo out of her purse and held it out to Perry Rhodan. "Hello, Mr. Rhodan. I wanted . . . I wanted . . ."

Rhodan looked at the picture, which showed the crew of the old *Stardust I*. "Where did you get that photo?"

"From my husband. He did not return. He was the only one who did come back from the moon with you. I wanted to talk to you about this. You were Clark's friend. . . ."

"Clark's friend? Are you Mrs. Fletcher?"

Anne Sloane, who was capable of telekinesis but otherwise lacked any necessary quality for a secret agent, particularly a strong will, nodded in affirmation with the last of her strength.

"She is lying!" stated John Marshall loud and clear.

Anne Sloane stared at the telepath with horror in her eyes. She no longer made any effort at continuing her pretense. Tears filled her eyes. "How do you know that I am lying?"

"Because I know your name is not Mrs. Fletcher but Anne Sloane, who has never been married. You were sent here by Allan D. Mercant and Colonel Kaats to spy on us. They selected you because a normal human being could never have passed through our energy screen around the base. You are a telekinetic mutant, aren't you?"

Anne Sloane could not bear to hear the truth about herself, and she began to cry bitterly.

"Help her, please!" commanded Rhodan. "Take her to my office!"

Anne Sloane was not bothered with any more questions until she had recovered from the shock of having been found out so rapidly. Rhodan had ordered a cup of coffee to be brought to her, a gesture that increased her inexplicable feeling of having found security at last.

Marshall whispered something into Rhodan's ear and Perry turned to the girl.

"Lieutenant Colonel Mercant recognized your special talents and sent you to us, didn't he?"

"You know he did. If I visualize what that young man, who never before laid eyes on me, has told about me, then I know that even the smartest secret agent wouldn't have the ghost of a chance with you. But how can that be? Colonel Kaats has always tried to make me believe that you have a few tricks up your sleeve but that your miserable little group doesn't amount to much otherwise."

"We are a small group as far as numbers go. That's true. But we are far from being miserable, Miss Sloane! The young man who made such an impression on you a little while ago is an excellent telepath. By the way, he just whispered to me that you never had a strong intention to spy on us when you came here. But you had a great desire just to come here and join us."

"That sounds like a silly excuse on my part, I'm afraid."

"It certainly appears that way, Miss Sloane. But we know that it is the truth. We can read your thoughts; we know exactly what you are thinking."

Anne closed her eyes. The feeling of having found a safe

harbor left her. Even without being a telepath, Rhodan could understand what seemed to upset her.

"I am familiar with the sensation of being exposed to the probing of a telepath. He penetrates into the last secret corner of your mind, and there is nothing left of any privacy in your life. Is that what disturbs you so?"

"Yes," she said with a small voice. "I believed I had found here something great—freedom at last. But now I realize I was wrong."

Perry Rhodan smiled gently. "We will restore your belief, Miss Sloane. You will be free here, the same way I have attained such freedom."

"How is it possible to protect yourself against his probing mind?" she wondered, gazing fearfully at John Marshall.

"We will teach you to erect a barrier around your thoughts. This can be done partly by a special technique and partly by psychostudies. You can learn it within a few weeks."

"Do you want me to stay here that long?"

"You can remain here as long as you wish. Forever, if you so desire."

Anne's answer was a mute smile.

To avoid any additional emotional shocks to Anne's delicate state of mind, Rhodan had suggested that John Marshall should not be around her for the time being. Dr. Haggard was put in charge of finding suitable quarters for her.

Perry Rhodan, master of the Third Power, set out again on his way to the factory sheds. But his mind was not on the work he had intended to do there. He was preoccupied with a new problem that had arisen, and he kept mulling it over in his mind, examining it from every possible angle.

Allan D. Mercant had sent her to the base! The Chief of the International Intelligence Agency. Would this man turn out to be a disappointment after all? Rhodan already looked upon him as an important figure in his own scheme of mankind's future. He had visited him in his headquarters under the Greenland ice and had received him here in the Gobi Desert as a mediator for the Western Powers. Something like sympathy had sprung up between the two of them. And now Mercant was sending a telekinetic to him as a spy. . . .

Rhodan was suddenly interrupted in his train of thought by an alarm signal coming from Khrest.

"Hello, Rhodan! Calling Perry Rhodan! Come at once to the Arkonide sphere! We have located new activity in the moon's orbital path."

Rhodan activated a switch on his all purpose transporter suit, which let him bridge the thousand feet to the space sphere immediately and without any effort. He landed in the air lock and ran at once to the center where Khrest was stationed.

"What have you located? Where exactly? Is that another invasion, do you think? So soon? This comes at the worst possible moment for us!"

"It is too early to say anything definite yet. We found signs of some activity up there. But it was to be expected that the Fantan people would bring up reinforcements any day now. We knew that ever since their first attempt failed."

Rhodan's decision came instantaneously. "We will investigate the situation and attack them if it seems advisable. We can't risk waiting for them to attack us here on Earth! Neither the Arkonides nor the population of this world can afford it. Will you permit me to use your ship again?"

Khrest was so much now under the spell of Rhodan's personality that he interpreted Rhodan's request as an order. A brief sign with his hand expressed his willingness to relinquish all authority to the Earthling.

Sirens sounded the alarm, mobilizing the small garrison of the Third Power. Rhodan issued commands that could be heard everywhere inside the energy dome.

"Mr. Klein and Mr. Li Tschai-tung report to me at the space sphere command center. Peter Kosnow will be in charge of radio communication. All other personnel continue working according to schedule. No change in plan for the robot force. Get ready to start!"

The Arkonide sphere rose vertically, passing through the momentarily lifted energy barrier. Immediately after lift-off the spaceship developed an acceleration of fifty G's with the help of its fully synchronized antigrav, which kept those inside from feeling any effects from the acceleration.

They reached the orbital path of the moon in less than one hour. Only the hypnoschooled minds of Rhodan and Khrest could grasp the furiously fast changing position data supplied by the robot radar system. Rhodan's and Khrest's reaction time exceeded the human norm by five hundred times. Thus it was understandable when Klein begged them to slow down the flight.

Rhodan complied with this wish, for he had found out by then that the speed with which the enemy ship was following the moon in its orbital path was considerably slower than their own. Once again Rhodan applied the effect of the antigrav, but this time it had to even out the braking force. Then they were able to observe the enemy craft clear and steady on their video screen.

"But this spaceship isn't spindle shaped! These can't be the Fantan people after all!" exclaimed Li Tschai-tung. "What do you think of this, Khrest?"

"This spaceship is oval shaped. Therefore, it cannot be of Arkonide origin. However, my race has had more enemies than friends during the past centuries. This leads me to the conclusion that according to the laws of chance we should be facing here a hostile force."

Perry Rhodan maneuvered the space sphere into a favorable position for attack, then applied a testing ray.

"They are surrounded by an energy screen. If we knew its strength . . ."

This was merely a rhetorical remark, for Rhodan was already busy evaluating the testing ray's results. "If we transform the enemy craft into pure energy, the world's population will acquire a new miniature sun in the skies. It would be specious at this point to calculate in detail what the meterological consequences of such a new star on our horizon would be, but it would inevitably lead to enormous catastrophes in our weather."

"The oval shaped ship has intensified its energy screen because we have arrived in its vicinity," explained Khrest. The enemy crew certainly knows that they are invulnerable now."

"We must employ more conventional weapons if we want to be successful in our attack," mused Rhodan. "Such as an explosion inside the hostile ship. I am sure that the explosive force released by ten tons of TNT would be sufficient to render the oval ship harmless."

"I can appreciate your desire, but it is impossible to execute this wish of yours unless you can come up with some additional trick."

"I have already figured out that trick," replied Rhodan dryly. "Part of it will be to begin now feigning some frontal attacks. I want them to believe that this is the only method of attack in our strategy."

The Arkonide sphere suddenly jumped ahead and closed in on the enemy ship. The distance between the two opponents was now diminished to nine thousand miles. Rhodan set up a barrage of energy rays that produced a colorful pyrotechnical display on the enemy's energy barrier but could not penetrate it. The fake attack had yet another unexpected result—the oval shaped craft disappeared suddenly from view, not by changing over into paraspace or by creating an invisible field through artificial curvature of space; it simply accelerated its speed by three thousand feet per second and thus disappeared as a shrinking dot in the vastness of the universe.

Everyone's reaction to this disappearing act was one of utmost surprise. Even Rhodan and Khrest could not escape being totally startled.

"Have you ever seen a spaceship with such powerful engines?"

Khrest was at a loss. "We don't know what is going on at the center of the galaxy while we are away from there. Every day might bring further technical progress. There are several races capable of such scientific achievements. And there are quite a few besides for whom oval shaped spaceships are characteristic. We need more information. I suggest we return and consult the positronic brain at the Gobi Desert base."

Perry Rhodan guided the Arkonide sphere back to Earth. The thought of having at least chased away the opponent made him hope he had gained valuable time.

They landed at the Gobi Desert base and proceeded at once toward the hall housing the positronic brain.

But this day really seemed to be hexed. Peter Kosnow

called the group and asked to see Rhodan in a most urgent matter.

"What on Earth is happening now?"

"There is someone waiting for you outside the energy screen who insists on talking to you personally, sir. He arrived there half an hour ago by plane. He sent the plane back again, informing me that he would no longer have any need for it. He intends to be your guest for quite some time to come."

"Did he say who he is?"

"He would not tell me his name. Just that he is a good friend of yours, Mr. Rhodan."

"Let him through the barrier and bring him to my office. Strict surveillance, of course."

Rhodan told his companions that he would join them at the robot brain within half an hour. Then he went to his bungalow to await the unknown visitor.

Kosnow lifted the energy screen for a few seconds and sent a robot car to pick up the visitor. When the mysterious visitor was brought to him Kosnow was amazed.

"Lieutenant Colonel Mercant! Where are you coming from?"

"Straight from my headquarters in Greenland, Kosnow. Glad to see you here!"

The Russian reacted rather reticently to this friendly greeting. "Will you follow me, please, sir. Mr. Rhodan is expecting you."

"The pleasure does not seem to be mutual," snapped Mercant.

Kosnow did not reply. He led Mercant to Rhodan's office, where a similar scene ranging from cordiality to cool restraint took place. But here Mercant felt that an explanation was due.

". . . Naturally you can imagine that this is not just a pleasure trip for me. I have quite valid reasons for coming to see you here. But at our last meeting you reacted much more frankly and cordially toward me. I understand, of course, your change of attitude. But I am not hiding any tricks up my sleeve. I want to be totally sincere with you. You resent the affair with Anne Sloane; isn't that so?"

"Sure," Rhodan confirmed abruptly.

Mercant continued, "I realized that Anne Sloane could never be depended on to any great extent. At least, not for the task that Kaats had imagined. If I nevertheless entrusted the girl with that mission, you could have guessed where my sympathies lie."

"Don't tell me that your sympathies lie with me. I am not receptive today to any flatteries."

"Please, don't take everything personally, Mr. Rhodan. I came here because of my sympathies for the Third Power. And this again is not based on personal preferences. I am deeply concerned with the fate of mankind and their future welfare. And since I am convinced that you alone are capable of fending off the invasion from outer space, I have decided to visit you here."

"You plan to stay here for a while?"

"That is up to you, Mr. Rhodan."

Rhodan had not heard such frank words for a long time. He appreciated Mercant's attitude.

"That decision will have to be made later. I will have someone take you to your quarters. Later we can discuss things more thoroughly. Will you excuse me now? I have something urgent to see to."

"I observed your landing with the Arkonide space sphere a while ago. I don't doubt the importance of your errand. But please, do listen for just a moment to what I have to tell you. It is not a whim that made me come to see you just at this particular time."

With these words Mercant put a large briefcase on the table and opened it. Rhodan could not object any more. He saw the strange limbs that his visitor had brought along from the icy wastes of Greenland. He intuitively felt the importance of these fragments.

"What is that, Mercant?"

"That is what I would like to find out from you or from Khrest. We located a strange igloolike structure far to the north of the Umanak Fjord. When we exploded it we discovered the remains of some unknown life form. We are sure it is extraterrestrial."

At once Perry Rhodan summoned Khrest, Marshall, Haggard and Thora via intercom to his room. Shortly afterward the three men entered. Thora failed to answer Rhodan's call.

Brief introductions were followed by Allan D. Mercant's detailed report of the latest events in Greenland. Captain Zimmerman's fate and the corpus delecti gave rise to tremendous excitement among the men. No one any longer doubted that the world had arrived at an important turn in its future fate. Questioning glances were directed at Khrest.

"It has become superfluous to consult the positronic brain, for here lies our answer. Captain Zimmerman was no turncoat or traitor, Mr. Mercant. He was a victim of these creatures."

"These aren't the Fantan people?"

"No. These creatures are far more dangerous and treacherous. The emergency signal that was automatically released at the destruction of our exploratory space vessel on the moon has obviously drawn the attention of a large number of higher intelligences to this sector of the universe. You must resign yourselves to the fact that the position of Earth in the galaxy has finally become known. This will inevitably lead some races, motivated by curiosity, greed or destructive instincts, to investigate this solar system. First came the Fantan people and then the M.S. But the M.S. always travel in crowds, and wherever one of them is sighted you must reckon on the presence of others of their kind."

"What do you mean by the M.S.?"

"I'll try to explain this with Captain Zimmerman's example. The name of these creatures cannot be pronounced in the Arkonide language because of a total absence of vowels. We simply call them therefore the M.S., short for Mind Snatchers. These beings are the most feared enemies of our empire. A natural, inborn capacity permits their minds to leave their own individual bodies and to take possession of any other living creature's body. That means that their ego can stay for a very long time inside some other being's body, whose mind in turn has been transferred to the vacated shell of the M.S. A simple case of involuntary mind swapping. Captain Zimmerman must have encountered such an M.S. during his routine flight over

Greenland. When he came to see you, Mr. Mercant, he had already been seized by the ego of the M.S. This creature's body was resting far to the north under the mysterious igloolike structure, where it was well protected and served as a painful prison for Zimmerman's mind.

"Absolutely horrible!" shuddered Dr. Haggard. "Would you know whether this strange power is coupled with metabolical faculties?"

"You are thinking of organic imitation or reconstruction, Dr. Haggard. You wonder if the M.S. take over the host's body, including its own protoplasm. No, not at all. There is no alteration as far as the metabolism is concerned. But having one's body taken over by some foreign mind seems diabolical enough to me."

Everyone present agreed fully with Khrest's opinion. Only Dr. Haggard seemed to go one step further, and even as the additional thought occurred to him he made an involuntary move away from Mercant. Just as swiftly and without conscious deliberation he whipped out a pistol and pointed it at Allan D. Mercant.

"We are discussing the M.S., gentlemen, but aren't we forgetting at the same time that Mercant was with Zimmerman shortly before he died?"

Khrest grasped at once what was on Haggard's mind and made a reassuring gesture to him. "You can put your gun away, Dr. Haggard. An M.S. can jump only from his own body over to that of another person. For every new exchange they must first return to their own bodies. Therefore, it was impossible that the M.S. seized Mercant's body when Zimmerman died."

"What happened then to the mind of the M.S.? Where is it now?"

"The M.S. died the same instant as Captain Zimmerman. Certain preparations are necessary before it can return to its own body. A kind of gathering of strength. This limitation is one of the few points where we can attack them successfully."

"Then both are dead? Zimmerman and the M.S.?"

Khrest confirmed Dr. Haggard's assumption.

"Wouldn't it be most probable that what happened to

Zimmerman was not an isolated case?" Mercant asked Khrest.

"Most likely, Mr. Mercant. I share your suspicions. The situation might be far more serious than we realize. Zimmerman's case proves that the M.S. have been active on Earth for the last two to three days. Many cases of mind swapping might have occurred. I would recommend that you warn all mankind, for everyone becomes suspect from now on. Any absurd or misanthropic act should be reported at once."

"Do you realize what that would mean?" warned Rhodan.

Khrest answered, "Panic! Widespread panic! If you should find some better solution I would suggest you adopt it, Rhodan."

"Another question, Khrest. Is it necessary for the M.S. to be physically close to their intended victims, or can they jump from great distances?"

"They are capable of both. If their aim is difficult because their target is among many other beings, then they usually approach it quite close before they jump. But if their prey should go for a walk alone in the middle of the Gobi Desert, they might, if need be, operate over a distance of several thousand miles—even from a spaceship hovering out in space."

An hour later, Rhodan told Mercant and Dr. Haggard, who had remained behind in his office, "Tako has sent a message via radio. They are bringing thirteen mutants along with them."

"Mutants?" questioned Mercant.

"Mutants for the Third Power, Mr. Mercant. People like yourself. The crew to man our station. The number of inhabitants in our new state will remain severely limited for a long time. As a result we will have to substitute quality for quantity. Only the best and most capable persons will do for citizenship and service in our domain. I am about to found the Secret Mutant Corps. A troop smaller and less conspicuous than any other but also faster, stronger and more reliable."

"I admire you, Rhodan. Yes indeed! You have made

up my mind for me. I feel that you have confidence in my abilities. May I join your troop?"

"I was hoping for this request, Mr. Mercant!"

They sealed Mercant's entry into the Third Power with a firm handshake.

A voice broke in on the intercom, announcing that Tako's transport plane was about to land.

Rhodan arrived at the landing strip as the plane touched down. Tako was the first person off the plane.

"Mission accomplished, sir! Twelve mutants with strong deviations from the norm on board. They are not in a very friendly mood, as you can imagine. Most of them want the first chance they get to have you prosecuted by an international court of law for kidnapping!"

"Thank you, Tako," replied Rhodan with a cryptic smile. "Just see to it that they get off the plane now. But what happened to the thirteenth mutant you reported earlier?"

"He will be arriving with Reginald Bell. Bell is flying him directly from Germany to the base. They should be here by this afternoon."

"Fine! Now let's welcome our new arrivals."

The first meeting between Rhodan and the mutants turned out to be far less dramatic than the latter had imagined. Filled with outrage they exited from the machine, talking excitedly with each other. But their noisy indignation was soon silenced. As soon as they came close to where Rhodan was waiting for them, they stopped their chatter.

"Welcome, ladies and gentlemen!" Rhodan greeted them. "You will be the guests of the Third Power. I want to apologize for the unusual manner we had to use in inviting you here. But you may rest assured that none of you will be deprived of personal freedom here in any way. You will be lodged in our most comfortable quarters, without any cost to you. During your stay with us you will have the opportunity to participate for several hours daily in a very interesting hypnotraining course, designed to reveal and develop your true mental capacities. You will be able to discover your true mental potential for yourselves! You will soon find out how little you have been informed about the extent of your own abilities. Consider this training as an entertaining but harmless game, from which you will profit. In one week I will meet you again and discuss any questions you might have. At the same time this plane will be ready to return each to his home again."

Perry Rhodan then shook hands with each of the dozen mutants, with a friendly word for each of them, and then left them in the care of an already well tried and trusted team consisting of Dr. Haggard, Dr. Manoli and John Marshall, the telepath.

Rhodan was waiting for his friend Bell's arrival. But this day's surprising events had not yet come to an end. While they were sitting at lunch a new warning came from Khrest.

"M.S. ship approaching again from outer space. Rotating in the same orbit as this morning. You promised to prepare some trick, Rhodan, if they ever showed up again. Now is the time!"

Perry Rhodan swallowed his last bite, jumped up and yelled into the intercom. "Don't you worry! I have something ready for them out there. This is our last hope. If this trick should fail, then all mankind might perish. This trick is going to work, because it simply has to!"

He ended by summoning Tako to the Arkonide spaceship. "Hello, Tako. Report to the space sphere immediately. We start in one minute!"

Perry Rhodan had always been a special kind of human being, and since he had undergone the Arkonide hypnotraining he had turned into a veritable genius. But little did even he guess at this moment what service he was rendering the Third Power as well as himself by acting so swiftly to put his well conceived trick in action.

The barrier fell. The sphere lifted off vertically. The barrier closed behind them. Acceleration, 150 feet per second, repeating the old game, the ever new dream flight of man to the moon. Earth to the moon in under one hour!

Turning into the satellite's orbital path, overcoming the horrendous centrifugal force; only then application of the braking energy. Perry Rhodan's movements and orders were brief and to the point. There was not even a wasted breath.

They were driven by the feeling that it was either the

aliens or Earth. And they were determined that Earth would be victorious.

Tako Kakuta was about to enter the small space module, not more than fifteen feet in length. He had been briefed by Rhodan in detail how to carry out his special mission. Now he was passing through the air lock, when Rhodan received a radioed message coming from the Gobi Desert base.

It was Kosnow who sent the bad news. "Calling Rhodan! I have just received an S.O.S. from Reginald Bell. He is approaching the energy dome in his airplane. He is complaining about an unbearable headache and requests immediate help. He has lost control over his engine. What shall we do? Go to his assistance?"

"Caution! M.S.!" called out Khrest.

"Connect me directly with Reg! I want to talk to him myself! . . . Hello, Reg! Can you hear me?"

"Perry, help me! I can't think any more. I don't know what's the matter with me—"

Rhodan's order to Tako: "Detach the space module at once and try teleportation within the next ten seconds!"

Rhodan's reply to Bell: "Resist, Reg! Keep resisting! This is not just a headache! You are being attacked by an alien mind trying to invade your body. We are out in the moon's orbit and are attacking the enemy this very moment. Can you hear me, Reg? Answer, please!"

"Perry! I can't bear it any longer! My head seems to be bursting. I—"

"Pull yourself together! You are stronger than they are. You have the Arkonide hypnoschooled mind! You possess a strong willpower! If you give in now, you will be lost. They want to devour your ego! Hold out, Reg! Just another minute now . . . another half a minute! Then you will have overcome it all. . . ."

Rhodan made promises that he was not yet sure of being able to fulfill. All depended now on the outcome of his trick, the strategical move designed to defeat the invading M.S.

Rhodan's first attack that morning had established that pure physical or energetical force applied from the outside was ineffective. The M.S. energy screen was too powerful.

But how powerful would that screen be if the M.S. believed themselves safe from attack? Everything hinged on that question.

After Tako Kakuta, the Japanese teleporter, had detached his spaceboat from the gigantic Arkonide space sphere, he approached the M.S. spaceship, assuming the same speed with which they were traveling, trailing after the moon. At the same time the Arkonide space sphere resumed a feigned attack with energy missile rays that were, of course, ineffective. Then they made a turn about and pretended to withdraw toward Earth.

The first part of Rhodan's plan succeeded.

The M.S. absorbed the light bombardment and did not react by disappearing hurriedly into the depths of space. There was a valid reason for this—they were trying to take over Reginald Bell's body. Therefore, they had to stay where they were and could not abandon their current position.

This was Tako's chance to teletransport himself.

As soon as the Arkonide ship had left the vicinity of the M.S., the latter's state of extreme alertness was relaxed. Tako's boat was too small to be located right away.

The Japanese needed fifteen seconds to achieve exactly the same speed as the opponent's ship. There was still 4,000 miles between them.

Then he jumped . . .

. . . and landed exactly in the middle of the enemy's command center.

The initial moment of surprise was sufficient for Tako to light his bomb. Then he teleported immediately back into his space module, where he watched the ensuing explosion of the oval shaped spacecraft.

Many experienced the explosion together with Tako—the crew of the space sphere, those in the ground station in the Gobi Desert, and especially Reginald Bell, who was suddenly and miraculously relieved of any pain and discomfort. He managed a safe landing of his plane with his passenger from Germany.

One week later.

The reports of Rhodan's new victory over the hostile invaders from space spread like wildfire over the globe. Everywhere people felt a new surge of sympathy for the Third Power.

In the meantime one of the strangest training courses ever to take place in mankind's history neared its end in the Gobi Desert base. All the inhabitants of the base had assembled in a big meeting hall that had been constructed by the robot workers. There was not a trace left of the outrage that the kidnapped persons' faces had shown one week earlier.

". . . and this brings me to the end of my talk, ladies and gentlemen," said Rhodan. "All of you have given me proof of your confidence in me to an extent that I had hardly hoped for. I had promised to return you to your homes again after this week's training. Of course, you will be able to go on leave at regular intervals, now that all of you without exception have decided to enter the service of the Third Power. The hypnobloc will prevent you from divulging any secrets while you are away on your vacations. Now, would you all rise, please, ladies and gentlemen. Herewith you will pledge yourselves for the rest of your lives to serve in the Secret Mutant Corps of the Third Power. This corps numbers now eighteen charter members. Each of you has demonstrated to my satisfaction that you have understood the historical impact of our new state seen from a cosmic point of view. You are aware of the capabilities of mankind up to this date, which were first enlarged with the maiden flight of *Stardust I*. You have experienced the sense of expectation that seized man when for the first time the gate to the universe was breached. You know that soon we will penetrate the deep secrets that no inhabitant of this planet even dared think about just a few years ago. You will become the nucleus of the elite group that will have to deal with and conquer all the future problems we are bound to encounter when we go out into space. It is up to you whether mankind's new venture turns into a nightmare or a blessing. Thank you."

The crowd soon dispersed, and Rhodan noticed with displeasure that Thora had been one of the first to leave.

"What's eating her?" he asked Khrest. "I thought I had come a bit closer to her. It's even been possible to have a sensible discussion with her lately. She even unbent enough to display some friendly emotions toward me. But ever since last week she won't talk to me and avoids me whenever possible."

"Ever since last week?" Khrest smiled with amusement. "Don't you remember what happened a week ago?"

"Well, a lot happened that memorable day. It was hot, the M.S. tried to invade us, Mercant came to visit, the affair with Reg . . ."

"You seem to forget how the day started. What was the first surprising event?"

"Miss Sloane arrived." Suddenly Rhodan arrived at an insight. "Do you mean to say that Thora is jealous of Anne?"

"She most certainly is!" laughed Khrest.

"Then we will forgive her all her nastiness, poor girl! A jealous Thora is about the best thing I could wish for to finish off a perfect day!"

Khrest left, and Rhodan thought he was alone in the room. But soon he became aware of someone else's presence, and he turned to see who it was. Far back in a corner he noticed Homer G. Adams. His dwarflike figure with the huge head bent forward made the Secretary of the Treasury of the Third Power look almost timid.

"Well, Adams, are you tired after your long trip from New York?"

The little man came nearer and shook his head energetically. "Such a trip from New York to the Gobi Desert is nothing really when you fly in one of your machines, Mr. Rhodan. No, I am bothered by something else. I am not the type of man to hide my light under a bushel. But a good financier is not the same as a mutant. And still you accepted me into your corps. Aren't you making a mistake here?"

Perry smiled. "Say, Mr. Adams, what is the cube of 2,369.7?"

"13,306,998,429.873."

"Did you figure that out just now?"

"Of course not! But you asked me the same question just a few days ago."

"And you remembered the result?"

"Why, naturally," said Adams as if this were a simple, everyday occurrence.

"You see," replied Rhodan, putting his hand on Adams's shoulder, "a normal person would never remember such a figure mentioned offhand in the course of an otherwise rather animated discussion. No one who has only five senses! But you did retain this figure. You have an eidetic memory. You are therefore fully entitled to join my Mutant Corps!"

The Radiant Dome

CHALLENGE FROM THE STARS . . .

Perry Rhodan had returned from the moon in Spaceship Stardust accompanied by two of the Arkonides. But the earth was on the verge of an atomic conflict. So Perry Rhodan, Peacelord of the Universe, threw an impregnable forcefield around the Stardust and declared his ship independent of the warring nations.

As he had hoped, the holocaust was temporarily averted by the more deadly threat of his allies from the stars; but could Perry Rhodan keep the peace long enough to persuade the Arkonides that mankind was fit to enter their galactic community?

THE RADIANT DOME is the second novel in the world's bestselling S.F. series. Don't miss Perry Rhodan's first cosmic adventure, ENTERPRISE STARDUST.

The Face in the Abyss

A remote valley hidden amid the towering peaks of the Andes and never before visited by civilised man is the scene of A. A. Merritt's classic novel of supernatural fantasy. The valley is inhabited by creatures long forgotten and races pledged to the resurrection of the glorious past.

Into this valley stumbles a young mining engineer, Nicholas Graydon. He defies the commands of the Snake-Mother's invisible but deadly servants and returns to the forbidden valley for the sake of Suarra, whom he loves. But Suarra can not be his until Graydon has persuaded the Snake-Mother to free the land of Yu-Atlanchi from Nimir, the Shadow of Evil. And the way to the Snake-Mother is beset with perils. Such as Lantlu, rider of dinosoaurs; the Lizard men. And, of course, the Dark Lord himself.

Dwellers in the Mirage

Beneath the shimmering surface of a lake cradled in the desolate Alaskan mountains, the people of the Shadowed-Land waited for Dwayanu, the warrior hero who will bring back to the world the worship of Khalk'ru, the cruel, destructive octopus god whose appetites must be appeased by human sacrifice.

When Lief Langdon accidentally discovers the people beneath the valley floor, they welcome him as the reincarnation of Dwayanu. Slowly Langdon's personality is possessed by the pride and blood-lust of his warrior ancestor until he is driven by forces beyond his understanding or control to serve the evil power of Khalk'ru.

A classic of science fiction, DWELLERS IN THE MIRAGE weaves a powerful web of fantasy against a background of lost civilisations.

Enterprise Stardust

PERILOUS DAWN . . .

Major Perry Rhodan, commander of the spaceship STARDUST, found more than anyone had expected might exist on the moon — for he became the first man to make contact with another sentient race!

The Arkonides had come from a distant star, and they possessed a knowledge of science and philosophy that dwarfed mankind's knowledge.

But these enormously powerful alien beings refused to cooperate with the people of Earth . . unless Perry Rhodan could pass the most difficult test any human being had ever faced . . .

ENTERPRISE STARDUST is the first novel in the Perry Rhodan series which sold more than 70 million copies in Europe and America.